Willa let out a gasp, one she didn't have to feign. It could be coincidence, but clearly they wanted her to, at the very least, think they had her father. At the very worst, they knew enough about her father to replicate the things he would have carried on him. "Those are my father's. Where did you get that?"

He nodded at the second man. "Excuse us." Both men turned their backs on Willa and Holden. Willa wanted to run. Away, to save herself. At them, to get her father's belongings. But all she could do was stand next to this lake and breathe too hard, furiously fighting the tears that wanted to fall.

Someone did have her parents, and now they wanted her.

Suddenly Holden was close. Too close, his mouth practically brushing her ear. "The minute the third guy comes out of the trees..." Holden muttered so quietly she almost couldn't hear him. "Fight for your life." Then he slid the handle of a knife into her hand.

SHOT THROUGH THE HEART

NICOLE HELM

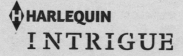

For the members of the Hermitage who always love a good farm animal.

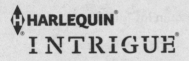

Recycling programs for this product may not exist in your area.

ISBN-13: 978-1-335-40180-9

Shot Through the Heart

Harlequin Enterprises ULC
22 Adelaide St. West, 40th Floor
Toronto, Ontario M5H 4E3, Canada
www.Harlequin.com

Printed in U.S.A.

Nicole Helm grew up with her nose in a book and the dream of one day becoming a writer. Luckily, after a few failed career choices, she gets to follow that dream—writing down-to-earth contemporary romance and romantic suspense. From farmers to cowboys, Midwest to *the* West, Nicole writes stories about people finding themselves and finding love in the process. She lives in Missouri with her husband and two sons and dreams of someday owning a barn.

Books by Nicole Helm

Harlequin Intrigue

A North Star Novel Series

Summer Stalker
Shot Through the Heart

A Badlands Cops Novel

South Dakota Showdown
Covert Complication
Backcountry Escape
Isolated Threat
Badlands Beware
Close Range Christmas

Carsons & Delaneys: Battle Tested

Wyoming Cowboy Marine
Wyoming Cowboy Sniper
Wyoming Cowboy Ranger
Wyoming Cowboy Bodyguard

Visit the Author Profile page at Harlequin.com.

CAST OF CHARACTERS

Holden Parker—North Star Group lead field operative on the hunt for a mysterious hit man.

Willa Zimmerman—Farmer trying to live a quiet life outside her parents' dangerous profession.

Sabrina Killian—North Star Group lead field operative. She flips a coin with Holden about which hit men they'll follow. Sabrina goes to Wyoming.

Shay—Current leader of the North Star Group.

Gabriel Saunders—North Star Group operative who helps Holden and Willa.

Elsie Rogers—Head of IT for the North Star Group.

Granger Macmillan—Former leader of the North Star Group who retired when he was injured, but sometimes he comes back to help on missions.

Chapter One

Holden Parker didn't need a mission to make him feel alive, but boy, it sure did help. Six weeks of investigating and not one minute of fieldwork had left him antsy and ready for action. *Real* action.

He hadn't joined the secretive North Star Group five years ago to wait around. He'd joined to do some good in the world.

For four years, he'd been able to stay in the field, constantly working to help bring down the Sons of the Badlands, a powerful gang that had run roughshod over the poorer communities in South Dakota.

In the past year, assignments had slowly dried up as the Sons had withered down to a noncriminal element. Holden knew he wasn't the only one who'd been afraid that was the end of North Star.

But the head of the group had come through with a new assignment a few weeks ago, and even though Holden had only been backup on that mission, it had been good to be in the field again. He was ready for more.

After six long weeks, Shay had *finally* called a

leader meeting for this morning. Which meant assignments were going to be doled out—real, in-the-
field assignments. Holden practically skipped to the
meeting room.

He met Sabrina Killian in the hallway and grinned,
because next to a mission and a nice, cold beer, there
were few things he enjoyed more than irritating Sabrina.

"You know it'll be me next. Shay's not sending
you out on a mission when you're still banged up,"
Holden said, nodding at her arm, which had spent six
weeks in a cast up until yesterday.

Holden himself felt much better with it gone. Then
he didn't have to feel guilty for not letting her finish
off the guys who'd ambushed her on their last mission. He knew she could have taken them, but he'd
also known her arm was seriously injured, so he'd
stepped in.

Sabrina had *not* thanked him.

She scowled at him now, and he knew she hadn't
forgiven him for it. Sabrina wasn't the forgiving sort.
He supposed, perversely, that's what he liked about
her. In a little-sister sort of way.

He saw too much of himself in Sabrina, which was
why he'd convinced the old head of North Star to give
her a job after she'd tried to beat him up in a seedy
South Dakota bar years ago. He'd seen too clearly a
person bent on destruction, just like he'd once been.

"We'll see," she muttered at him, walking shoulder to shoulder down the narrow hallway.

"Hey, remember when I saved your butt a few

weeks ago?" He slung his arm around her shoulder. She shrugged off the gesture before giving him a saccharine-sweet fake smile.

"Hey, remember when I kicked your butt a few years ago? Besides, if you'd given me a little more time, I could have taken those guys on my own. Fractured arm and all."

"Must be losing your touch. Want to try me now?" Holden offered, spreading his arms as if to offer her a free punch.

She tossed her long, dark ponytail over her shoulder. "When you've hung up your warped moral code about hitting women who were *this* close to being Navy SEALs, I'll fight you."

Before he could respond to that, someone cleared their throat.

Holden turned to see Shay standing in the entrance of the conference room, arms crossed, boss glare on her face. She'd been with North Star longer than any of them and had been tapped by their old leader to take over when he'd retired after a major injury almost two years ago.

Holden wouldn't say he liked her better than Granger McMillan, as he didn't really *like* having a boss, but what he did like about both his former boss and his current one was a shared desire to take down the bad guys. And a willingness to get the job done.

"Children," Shay said blandly. "If you'd enter so we could get this started?"

Sabrina sent Holden a haughty look, then sailed into the room in front of him. She took her usual chair, so Holden took his. He glanced at the empty one next to him. Reece wouldn't be coming to this meeting. Or any following meetings.

Reece Montgomery had quit. Left North Star for domestic bliss. Holden tried not to think about it, because the whole thing gave him the creeps. That a contained and hard man like Reece Montgomery could be undone by some innkeeper and her son was a bit *terrifying*.

Holden had no desire to be taken down in such a way. Ever.

Elsie Rogers sat at her computer in the corner tapping away, and at least some things would stay the same. As head of IT, Elsie barely ever left the digital light of her computer screen, and Holden doubted she ever would.

But Shay was going to have to promote one of the lower field operatives to replace Reece. It had been six weeks and she hadn't done it. And no one had pressured her to. Holden knew he should. He was now the senior field operative, after all. But he kept his mouth shut instead. They'd had enough change the past few years.

"What we have in the wake of the whole situation from a few weeks ago is two highly dangerous weapons in the hands of two highly dangerous individuals," Shay began, standing next to Elsie as she spoke to him and Sabrina.

"So, let's go," Holden said.

"As if anything is that simple. From what our

friends at the FBI can figure, we've just tangled with a highly specialized, complicated death machine."

"I thought it was a weapons dealer," Sabrina said with a frown.

They'd taken down a group selling black-market weapons to the wrong kind of people six weeks ago. The group had been thoroughly dismantled as far as Holden knew.

"Turns out, the weapons being supplied were only a small cog in a much bigger machine. Which means they'll just replace their weapons dealer. The FBI is putting a team on finding out more about this machine, but our job is much more urgent. While the FBI is trying to smoke out the head of the big group, we've got to stop two different hit men. Before we fully took down the weapons-dealer group, they shipped off two untraceable, highly powerful guns—and distributed them to two ghosts. And I do mean ghosts."

"Sounds like a challenge," Holden said, kicking back in his chair and balancing it on two legs. Man, he was ready for a challenge after all this downtime and *thinking*.

"Two hit men. Two guns that can make a joke out of Kevlar. We don't know who the hit men are. We don't know who the targets are. We don't even know how much time we have before they act. We know nothing. Except the guns themselves. The first lead we've gotten, thanks to Elsie's tireless work, is the delivery of ammunition for our weapon to two different PO boxes. Each equally untraceable, as the owners don't exist and security footage gives next to nothing away."

"So there's video of the ammunition being picked up?" Sabrina asked.

"Elsie's hacked what she can, and I'll show you that in a moment. Either way, you're going to split up and scout each address out. Our first target is Wilson, Wyoming. This is the only video we have of our suspect retrieving the package from the PO box."

A grainy security feed showed up on the big screen on the wall in front of them. A man dressed head to toe for winter weather walked over to one of the boxes. He kept his head completely turned away from the camera, blocking a row of boxes from view. He was wearing too many clothes to make out any sort of defining characteristic.

"A bit overdressed, isn't he?" Holden murmured.

"It's still cold enough at the upper elevations, but you're right. Seems odd. Especially since we know what's in the package. And what makes it more shady…" Shay nodded to Elsie, and another grainy video clicked on.

This video was similarly set up to the first, but definitely a different post office. "Evening, Nebraska."

Another person, dressed a bit heavily for a summer afternoon, came in in much the same way the man from the earlier video had. Too many clothes to make out defining characteristics, face kept pointed away from the camera, blocking the box as they opened it.

"That gives us two targets. I want you both on it. You can take a team if you want, but the first stages might be best done alone until you actually find the target. Though I'd want a team close by for backup. A full team completely in place before you take action."

"Define full team," Holden replied with a wide grin. He knew it would irritate Shay, and that was ever his goal. Because when she was irritated, she didn't get that far-off look in her eye that reminded him a bit too much of Granger before he'd been injured and quit North Star wholesale.

Holden didn't want to lose another boss. He didn't want to lose North Star and the missions that kept him employed and satisfied.

"We've got two people, at least, about to be killed, for reasons unknown to us. And that might only be the tip of the iceberg. Either way, we have very little to go on. It's important. But it's not more important than your own lives," Shay said sternly. Too serious these days. The weight of running North Star Group had definitely changed her.

Holden wasn't sure it was for the better.

"Don't you think that depends?" Sabrina asked.

Shay fixed her with a hard look. "This is a dangerous mission. You're risking your life by taking it on, but that doesn't mean you have to play hero."

"How would we live with ourselves if we didn't?" Holden asked, with none of his usual humor or joking. He'd joined the secretive North Star Group as a way out of the gang he'd gotten himself mixed up with. He'd joined to take down the people who'd lied to him and hurt him when he'd been at his weakest, angriest and most vulnerable. He'd joined to be the good guy instead of the bad guy. Mostly thanks to Granger McMillan.

Now, the Sons of the Badlands had been eradicated. As much as Holden was proud to have been a part of it, it didn't mean his need to erase all the bad he'd done had disappeared. Or ever would.

Shay got that *look* on her face that Holden didn't want to parse or think on. It was too much emotion, too much *change*. They didn't need it. They needed to act.

Holden turned to Sabrina as the same time she turned to him. In unison, they said the exact same thing to each other. "You take Nebraska."

"Not a snowball's chance in flat prairie hell," Holden replied.

Sabrina dug a coin out of her pocket. "Flip for it?"

"Who carries change around?"

"I found it yesterday in the gym. Thought it'd be good luck. Come on. Call it in the air. You win, you choose where you want to go."

Holden shrugged and grinned. "Sure. You should know luck always falls on my side."

She flipped the coin, and Holden called heads. When it landed tails, he muttered an oath.

Sabrina widened her eyes and laid on the fake regret. "Oh dear. It looks like I get to pick, doesn't it?"

Before Holden could argue with her, Shay interrupted.

"All right. Sabrina, you're headed to the Tetons. Holden, that means Nebraska for you."

Sabrina reached over and slapped him on the back. "Don't worry. I'll send you pictures of the mountains."

"Great," Holden muttered.

No, he didn't want to go to Nebraska, but hey, a mission was a mission. He'd be glad for it. Flat prairie and all.

NEBRASKA WASN'T QUITE the hell Holden had imagined, but it wasn't exactly a dream either. It wasn't all flat. In fact, there were some interesting rock formations that reminded him of South Dakota, where he'd grown up.

Which brought up feelings of nostalgia, regret and a determination to complete his mission and get back to Wyoming headquarters. Ideally before Sabrina did, so he could be deployed to the Tetons and irritate her in the process.

Sabrina's constant text messages of the picturesque Teton range was a constant reminder there were a lot prettier places in the world than Evening, Nebraska. This place was *all* small town. Lots of farms. Lots of flat, even with the occasional rock formation.

The town of Evening was minuscule. Made up mostly of a brief Main Street with a handful of businesses clearly kept alive only by a farming population that didn't have anywhere else to go for mail, banking or necessities.

The post office was a stone square of a historic building. Outside, there was a plaque that said it was on the National Historical Register and that it had been built in 1875. Inside, the lobby would *maybe* fit five people.

He'd been watching for a few days now. Inside, there was a small wall of PO boxes, and a counter where a friendly enough woman worked every day from nine in the morning until she closed down the entire building to take her lunch break from noon to one. She'd be back at one on the dot and stay open until four.

It was clear from moment one she did not trust strangers or appreciate any of Holden's charm. Still, she answered his questions. Though it had only been to say she had no recollection of a stranger renting or using PO box 10. In fact, she acted as if that particular PO box hadn't been rented in years.

Holden didn't think she was lying, but that meant someone had gone through a lot of trouble to know which PO boxes were empty, and how to break into a PO box. Quickly, too. The security video Elsie had hacked into had showed the man in and out in under three minutes.

A ghost, as Shay had said. The slim positive side to a ghost was he likely thought he had ample time to take out his target. Which meant Holden had more time to find him first.

Holden hoped. Because otherwise this was a *very* dead end.

On his third day in Evening, Holden watched the post office from across the street, pretending to smoke a cigarette outside the small general store. He deleted yet another smug text from Sabrina and her picturesque assignment, then asked her if she'd gotten any closer to her target.

He smiled when she didn't respond. She was no closer than him. He wasn't *glad* they had zero luck, but he'd enjoy the chance to still beat her to solving his assignment first.

He scanned Main Street again. The chance of his target coming back was probably slim, but the chance of seeing him walking around, shopping at the general store or driving down the street? Well, it was possible.

Even in the middle of the day, things were pretty quiet in this small town. Every once in a while someone would walk by, go in and out of the businesses. Sometimes people drove by. Some stopped. Some didn't.

Holden would watch them all without them knowing. A skill he'd developed once, many years ago, picking pockets.

A rusty old truck rumbled to a stop in front of the post office, blocking his view. Holden frowned and tossed the cigarette in the trash can. Pretending to take a casual stroll, he moved across the street and then down the sidewalk as the driver got out of the truck and walked to the post office door. She wore an oversize coat, jeans streaked with dirt and a ratty-looking stocking cap over messy braided pigtails.

For half a second, he thought she might be a child, but she'd been driving. Besides, she was too tall and her face wasn't really childlike. Youngish. Early twenties, probably. She stepped inside, and Holden angled himself so he could watch her through the windowed door. She didn't stop and chat with the woman behind the counter like the rest of the patrons had done since he'd been watching.

He inched closer, keeping her in view, but he stopped short when he saw what she was doing.

She was pulling a few envelopes out of the exact mailbox he'd been watching. Number 10. He counted once, twice, then three times to make sure it was in fact the mailbox that supposedly nobody owned. The mailbox someone had ordered high-powered, black-market ammo to be delivered to.

Holden eyed the woman. Could she have been the overdressed person who'd gotten the ammo earlier in the week? He'd assumed it was a man, but...

Before she closed the door to the box, she looked back over her shoulder and locked eyes with him, as if she'd felt him watching.

Damn.

Holden smiled lazily. Looking away would bring more suspicion than being a creep. He hoped.

The woman looked back at her mailbox. Her coat collar and pigtails obscured her face, but he figured his best course of action was to stay here and then hit on her. She might remember his face, she might be weirded out, but hopefully she wouldn't think much of it beyond that.

Especially if *she* was his target.

After a few more moments, she walked out of the post office. She kept her eyes straight ahead on her truck and didn't give him a second glance.

"Hi there," he offered.

She didn't respond. Didn't look at him. She just walked by, going straight for her truck.

Hmm.

"I thought small-town folks were supposed to be friendly," he called after her.

She gave him one cold look, then slid into the driver's seat of her truck. When she drove away, Holden noted her license plate number, the direction she was going and the size of her tires, then backtracked to go find his car.

Chapter Two

Willa Zimmerman didn't like the creeping sensation
that she was being followed. She didn't *see* anyone
on the old, cracking county highway behind her, but
she'd been taught to never, *ever* ignore her instincts.

The man was following her.

She glanced at the pile of envelopes in her passenger seat. Messages from her parents were rarely
a *good* thing. But she wouldn't be able to determine
how bad things were until she was in the safety of
her own home.

"You'd think they could just leave me out of it,
Stanley," Willa muttered at the snoozing sheepdog
in the back seat. He didn't even lift his head to pretend to humor her. "Goats are better listeners," she
muttered, turning onto the long, winding gravel road
that would lead her home.

She checked her rearview mirror again. Still no
sign of the man, but she knew he was there.

She also knew he wouldn't get past a certain point. At
least not in one piece. Which was a slim comfort when
all she wanted was to be left alone to see to her farm.

She glanced at the letters again. No doubt there'd be a warning included. What Willa didn't know yet was the urgency or level of the warning. Part of her wanted to ignore the letters, ignore the man, ignore who and what her parents were and just…live this perfect life she'd built.

But no life was perfect without a little imperfect payment.

She bumped along the gravel road as her house came into view. Even with a threat in the ether, the sight of her house and barns and menagerie of animals made her smile. Maybe she couldn't have a normal life, but the abnormal one she'd built for herself was her idea of paradise.

Mostly.

She parked the truck at the end of the gravel lane and hopped out. Since she hadn't seen her follower, she likely had about five to ten minutes before he got a little surprise she'd have to tend to.

She opened the back door of the truck and urged Stanley out. He sighed heavily and took his sweet time jumping out and onto the ground below. Then he huffed out a breath as if offended he'd had to move.

"You're the one who wanted to go with," she told him as he lazily made his way for the house, where he'd no doubt find a place on the porch to sit and sleep some more.

The noises of goats, pigs, sheep and chickens filled the air as she shoved the letters into the over-size pocket of her ancient coat. The letter would be written in code, because her parents were nothing if not dramatic.

She really didn't want to face it. Maybe that wasn't fair, but as she moved toward the house, three more dogs coming to greet her with happy yips and jumps, she considered, not for the first time, ignoring her parents completely.

If she cut them off, couldn't she prevent their drama from touching *her* life?

Like always, a wave of guilt followed that thought. Then a pang of longing. Even though her parents weren't the farming type, when they weren't off on "vacation," she usually saw them once a week for dinner.

It was her only true human interaction. As much as she loved her animals, and her farm, a woman could only hold so many one-sided conversations with a goat before she started missing *human* companionship.

Willa shook her head. This was her life, and there was no use wishing it could be different. She took a seat on the porch stairs, and two cats immediately slunk out from under the porch to wind around her legs.

She opened the envelope then absently scratched Angela's soft head.

Dearest Willa,
    We're enjoying our trip and hope things are safe and sound at home. Give Yellow a big hug for us.
Love,
Mom and Dad

Yellow. Well, it was better than Red, Willa supposed. What would she do with all her animals if her parents ever gave her a code red? She had doubts she'd even be able to follow through.

Her parents would *not* like that.

The alarm sounded, and Willa sighed, squinting off into the distance. It would have to be taken care of, and quickly.

What she wouldn't give for a normal life.

HOLDEN STUDIED THE area around him as he drove. Farm, farm, farm. Flat waving grain or green fields dotted with cattle. It was a nice day, with puffy white clouds wafting in the bright blue sky. He had his windows rolled down and couldn't deny that it was…nice. Relaxing. A pretty drive on a pretty day.

He slowed at every turnoff. Mostly they were gravel roads, no names, but a mailbox and gate at the end of each. Some gates were closed, some open. Sometimes he saw farm machinery out in a field, or a house far off from the road, but sometimes the fields seemed completely devoid of humans' presence.

He couldn't decide if it was delightful or downright creepy. He'd grown up in South Dakota but had always lived in Sioux Falls—not exactly a bustling metropolis. But a city. Sure, the occasional trip to the Badlands and its eerie, isolated landscape had given him a taste for wide-open spaces. But it felt right there to look out and see something that appeared untouched by human hands.

Here it felt… Well, Holden couldn't quite put his finger on the words for what it felt like.

As he drove slowly, he studied each gravel lane for signs of a vehicle being driven down it recently—puffs of dust or fresh tracks in the little strip of grayish mud between road and gravel.

The first time he found both, he turned down the gravel without hesitation. He hadn't seen another soul on the drive out of Evening, or to Evening. Or *anywhere*.

The gravel road wound around, curving this way and that, following a creek, avoiding a large, seemingly out-of-place rock cropping. Holden kept his speed slow, pretending he was enjoying a leisurely country drive on a pretty day.

He kept his windows rolled down, listening for anything, eyes sharp and assessing the situation even as he let a fake, easy smile play on his face.

A prickle of unease went across the back of his neck, and Holden slowed to a complete stop. Something was off. And weird. The road didn't seem to lead anywhere.

He turned off the engine and scanned the area. He listened. There was a slight breeze and the smell of clover and cow pies in the air. It should have been off-putting, but something about it was so bucolic he found himself smiling.

It was the most silence that hadn't bothered him in…ever.

Then he heard a rooster crow. Followed by the

echoing *baa* of sheep? A few seconds later, a moo followed.

What kind of living hell had he fallen into?

He shook himself out of the odd mood, the odd reverie of *peace*, and turned the ignition so the engine of the car purred to life. He'd follow the road the rest of the way. He wasn't ignoring that gut feeling that something was off. He was just considering the possibility his gut feeling was born of being weirded out by picturesque American heartland.

The gravel road wound around another thicket of trees, and Holden could see the hint of a house or a barn between the trees. He slowed his car to an absolute crawl, keeping his eyes on the building through the trees.

The woman could have led him into a trap. Alternatively, she could be a complete and utter innocent bystander. But there was something about *all* this that had his instincts humming.

As he came around the corner, before he could fully get an idea if the building was a house or a barn, his car made a shuddering noise and the entire vehicle jerked, which caused him to yank the wheel, since he was gripping it hard and hadn't put his seat belt back on.

Somehow that small yank had the whole car tipping toward the slight hill to the left. If he tipped any farther, the whole car would flip, and then…

Holden had a split second of inner swearing before the whole world went dark.

He had no idea how much time passed before he

found himself blinking his eyes open. His vision was blurry, but the world around him was definitely dark. And…enclosed. He wasn't on the ground. Or in his car. He was lying on something…not soft, exactly, but not hard.

He blinked a few more times then tried to sit up, but as he tried to move his arm to leverage himself into a sitting position, he couldn't. At least not far.

Something clanged next to him, like a chain rattling against metal. He turned his head through the pounding pain in his temple to look at his arm. Around his wrist was a handcuff, connected to a long chain that was attached to the other handcuff, which was fasted around the metal frame of a rusty old bed.

Terror spurted through him for one debilitating second, but he forced himself to breathe. Think. He'd been in a few tough spots before. He'd gotten out of them. He wasn't dead, so he could get out of this one.

If he could figure out what on earth had happened.

He looked around him. He appeared to be in some kind of…barn. Very old, if the cracks between boards that made up the roof were anything to go by. The sides appeared to be made up of stones with more aging, warped boards stacked on top.

There seemed to be *some* light outside, but it was dim. It allowed him to make out his surroundings in shadow, making him think he must have been unconscious for a few hours at best.

And somehow he'd been moved into some horror-movie barn and chained to a rusty old bed with an uncomfortable mattress. He looked down at his feet.

They were chained to the bed frame as well. And in between his legs were two glowing eyes.

Holden tried to scramble out of the way, but of course he was *chained* by every limb to this creaky bed frame.

A door squeaked open, the screech of metal on metal making Holden wince. The animal between his legs began to paw at his knee.

"Oh, you're awake," the woman said. "I suppose that's a good thing." It was the woman from the post office. She looked perfectly calm, as if this was normal. She was still wearing the same outfit she'd worn at the post office, and she studied him with serious green eyes.

"I'm chained to a bed," he said, just in case she'd somehow stumbled upon him and didn't understand the situation.

"Mm." She tilted her head to the side, studying the bed below him. "Such as it is anyway."

"You chained me to a bed."

"Yes," she agreed, as if that wasn't *insanity*. "Seemed the safest option. Oh, Kelly. Don't be a pain." She walked over and picked up the creature between his legs. A cat. A very large, very fat cat.

She gently put the cat on the floor of the barn then turned to him. "So. Who are you?"

He glanced from the woman to the cat, who was sitting next to the woman's feet, creepy cat eyes squarely on him. "Who am *I?* You chained me to a bed in some dilapidated barn in the middle of nowhere."

She looked around the barn as if seeing it for the first time. "I admit it's a bit rough around the edges, but dilapidated is harsh, don't you think?"

"I…" Holden was left utterly speechless, a sensation he couldn't remember *ever* having.

He studied this woman. It was hard to believe she was some kind of ghost assassin, what with the farmer overalls and the fresh-faced beauty. Holden knew looks could be deceiving but still, her gaze was frank, wary, but not…cruel.

But regardless of who or what she was, she was obviously unbalanced. What with him being chained to a bed and all.

He closed his eyes for a moment. He had to get his wits about him. This jumbled, speechless feeling was a side effect of being knocked out, surely. Once he could get his mind in working order, he'd find a way to escape this.

She hadn't killed him, after all. He opened his eyes and frowned at her. As far as he knew, she hadn't even hurt him. She'd just…what exactly? Dragged him into a creaky old barn and chained him up?

"You probably need something to drink," the woman observed. She walked over to a little cabinet and grabbed what appeared to be a tin cup, like people used when camping. He couldn't move enough to see her as she walked farther into the barn, but he heard the groan and then whoosh of water running through a pipe.

When she returned to his field of vision, she had the cup in her hand and was studying the chains on his hands. She made a considering noise, then did something that allowed the chain to move more liberally against the metal frame. He was still chained to it, but he could lift his arm.

She handed him the cup. "You should probably drink all this. I don't know that it'll help the whole headwound thing, but you don't want to get dehydrated."

His brain clearly still wasn't working because all he could do was stare at her. Baffled. Utterly and completely baffled. "You dragged me into your creepy horror-show barn and chained me to a bed."

"You seem to be having a really hard time with that, but yes. That is what happened. Are you having, like…short-term memory loss?"

"Are you having a break with reality?"

She blinked and managed to somehow look offended. "No. But when some man follows me home from town and then tries to drive onto my pro— I think I have a right to defend m——

"I didn't do anything to you."

"You followed me. Like a stalker."

"So call the police."

Her expression changed. He couldn't read the change or what it meant, but it was almost like she'd clicked some new armor into place. "This'll do. Now. Drink the water."

She shoved the cup into his hand. He probably could have grabbed her arm. With the extra movement of the chains, he could probably debilitate her.

But all he could seem to do was curl his fingers around the cup she handed him.

Chapter Three

The man took the cup, but then he just lay there as if he wasn't quite sure what to do with it. Willa had bandaged up his head wound and the other cuts and scratches on him from his car accident while he'd been unconscious, but clearly he wasn't quite one hundred percent.

"You probably need to sit up to drink," she decided when he simply held on to the cup.

"How?"

She knew it was silly to feel sorry for someone clearly here to do her some harm, but she couldn't help it. He was injured and confused, and she *had* chained him to a bed in an old barn she mostly used for storage.

"I'll help you." She went around to the back of his head and grabbed his shoulders, pushing him up. She perched herself on the edge of the bed, letting his back lean against hers in an upright position so he could drink his water.

His back was warm, and she could feel the movements of his muscles as he lifted the cup to his mouth.

It was such a stark reminder of how isolated her life was. How devoid of any real human contact when her parents weren't home. Because she felt some odd relief inside herself to be touching another human being.

Get it together, Willa.

"Do you feel dizzy?" she asked, staring hard at the stone foundation of the barn's walls.

There was a pause. "No."

She found she didn't believe him. He was a big guy. Clearly very strong. The fact he hadn't tried to fight his way out of the chains showed he was either still out of sorts or smart enough to think his situation through first.

Willa still hadn't been able to think through her situation. After the security measures had been deployed when the man had crossed over onto her legal property, she'd gone out. He'd driven a small sedan, which had flipped at the impact of the device meant to pop a car's tires and maybe damage its undercarriage but not actually flip it.

She'd had to drag him out of the car and then back to the barn. After she'd searched the bag he'd had in the back seat. He had tactical gear, but only one gun. Not a particularly fancy one. None of it pointed at hired killer.

Her best guess was this man was here to kidnap her. She shouldn't be giving him water or asking after his head injury. She should be taking care of things.

Her parents would scold her for her soft heart, and then they'd worry over her more than they already did. It was half of why she hadn't sent a message their way. She wanted to handle this on her own. To prove to them she could be left alone to have this life she wanted.

She might be an adult, but she was connected to her parents no matter what any of them did. Their work left Willa a vulnerable target, and it had taken years to convince them she didn't have to bounce from place to place with them. She could build her own home on her own two feet and stay safe.

She'd sacrificed friends and relationships with pretty much anyone to have that freedom and independence. She wouldn't give it up just because this man didn't *seem* like a cold-blooded killer. Especially since she knew he very well could be.

"I don't suppose you're going to tell me what on earth is going on?" he said after a while. His voice was deep. Calm, sure. he sounded a little baffled, but not too out of it for a man who'd been unconscious for a few hours.

"I don't suppose you'll tell *me* what on earth is going on?" she returned. Because, truth be told, she wanted to tell him everything. She liked truth and honesty and clear-cut answers. She didn't want to play her parents' games.

But if this connected to them, she had to.

He sighed and didn't answer before taking another sip of his water.

"What's your name?" she asked.

This time his answer was a derisive snort.

She didn't mind that so much. "You can call me Willa."

"Willa what?"

This time it was her turn to snort derisively. "I could tell you, but then I'd have to kill you."

"Is that not the plan?"

"You're here and alive, aren't you?"

"Here," he repeated. "Chained to a bed in a horror film set come to life."

"It's not *that* bad," Willa returned. "It's just rustic. My other barn is much nicer. Well, it has to be, because that's where the animals live. The ones who don't live in the house with me, that is. Or, you know, are outside animals. Kelly here prefers this barn," she said, pointing at the cat, though she supposed from his angle behind her, he couldn't see her point.

He said nothing for a few more minutes. "Does it hurt?" she asked after a while.

"What? The lump on my head I can only assume is the size of another head?"

She shouldn't smile. She shouldn't be *enjoying* a conversation with a man who was here to hurt, threaten, kidnap or possibly even kill her. But it was just so nice to talk to someone who wouldn't only make animal noises in return.

Which, speak of the devil, was followed by the sounds of a goat bleating incessantly. Then said goat showed up in the barn opening.

"Dwight, why do you have to be so ornery?"

The goat bleated again, and Willa sighed. She had to carefully scoot away from the bed so the man wouldn't fall back down on the old, hard mattress. She tried to be gentle as she held his shoulders until he was back to a laying position.

She walked over to the doorway where Dwight stood. She turned back to the man. "I'll be back in a bit with dinner. And some new bandages."

He stared at her with steady blue eyes. She couldn't read his expression. She knew she should feel *some* fear, but she didn't really.

"So, you're just going to leave me locked up like this?" He frowned at her and the goat. "With whatever the hell that is roaming around?"

She studied the large man chained to the bed in her barn. "I suppose I am." What other choice did she have? "And this is a goat. His name is Dwight."

"I'm dreaming," he muttered to himself. "I'm in a hospital somewhere and this is some drug-induced coma dream."

"Hate to break it to you, but you're stone-cold awake. Don't worry. I'll be back in a bit, and Kelly will keep you company while I'm gone."

As if on cue, the cat jumped back on him—this time on his stomach instead of in between his legs. He let out an *oof*, as Kelly was not a small cat.

"You've got to be kidding me," the man muttered as Willa grabbed Dwight's collar and began dragging him back to his pen.

With a very out-of-place smile on her face.

HOLDEN STILL HELD out hope this was a really realistic dream, but that hope aside, he'd gotten his brain in gear enough to start fiddling with the chains. It wouldn't take much to break his way out of these.

If the cat stopped trying to sit directly on his face, like some kind of demon bent on his death by suffocation.

He jerked his head to the right, trying to get the cat dislodged, but that only sent a throbbing, stabbing ache through his temple. He groaned in pain, which finally dislodged the cat.

She jumped off him gracefully, then glared up at him as if he'd inconvenienced *her.* "Ease up on the attitude, princess. I could skin you alive if I wanted to."

The cat clearly didn't fear his threats, as she lifted one paw to her mouth and delicately began to clean it.

Holden blew out a breath. He had some ideas on how to break out, but he'd wait. The woman had said she'd come back with dinner. So, he'd hold tight until after, when she left and closed the door for the night.

She wasn't going to kill him…he thought. So he could bide his time.

The woman—Willa, if that was her real name— had left the barn door open. So he'd been able to watch night fall. Birds flew in and out. He saw a trio of dogs run by at one point. He'd heard chickens and sheep.

And he hadn't seen one hint that any other *human* being lived anywhere near here.

"I'm in an insane asylum. I'm in hell. Maybe this is purgatory," he said aloud, if only to hear himself speak and try to convince himself it wasn't some weird dream.

As if on cue, Willa appeared in the doorway, carrying a little tray and a lantern. She was too pretty for it to be purgatory. Which was not a productive thought—at all.

"I brought you some dinner," she announced, her voice friendly and warm, as if this was *normal*.

Holden didn't bother to move. "Am I going to be unchained to eat, warden?"

"No, I don't think so."

"Then what? You're going to feed me?"

She made an odd noise—like she'd been trying to snort derisively but a squeak came out instead. "Um, *no*." She came to stand next to the bed, still holding the tray and staring down at him as if she was considering *how* he was going to eat.

"So, what are you going to do?" he asked, trying not to sound as irritable as he felt. Maybe her cheeriness was an act, but maybe it was something he could use to get what he wanted. If he kept his charm in place. A tall order right now.

She sighed. "It's quite a conundrum, isn't it? It'd help if you told me who you are and what you're doing."

"Would you believe me if I did?"

She considered that. "I guess it depends. What's your name?"

She had an odd, open conversational manner about her. It kept him on uneven footing. Or maybe that was just the head injury that had his real name slipping out. "Holden."

"Holden," she repeated. "Well, that doesn't sound made up."

"Gee. Thanks."

Her mouth curved. It made no sense she was smiling. It made even less sense he wanted to smile back. This woman had *chained him to a bed*. While he had a *head injury*. From some sort of...setup. She had to have had something to do with his car flipping.

Somehow.

She bent down and put the tray on the floor. He could see a plate with a sandwich, an apple, a baggie full of Goldfish crackers and a water bottle.

"Who *are* you?"

She smiled up at him, the stray tendrils that had fallen out of her pigtails creating a reddish curtain over her face. "I told you my name is Willa."

"That hardly explains why a seemingly perfectly nice woman booby-trapped my car, dragged me into a godforsaken shed and chained me to a bed from the 1800s."

"The bed is more likely 1950s. Barn, yeah, 1800s. Probably 1875, if I had to guess. Kind of amazing, isn't it? Imagine the history this place has seen. I wish whoever owned it before me had kept it in better shape. I'd fix it up, but it seems such a travesty to mess with what's always been here. I always think I'll do some research and see who owned the place before I did, but I never seem to get around to it."

"Am I on drugs?" Maybe she was poisoning him. Because surely he wasn't chained to a bed while a pretty woman talked about the history of the building he was being held prisoner in.

"You're probably hungry," she said. She clicked something on his chain that gave him more range of motion again. Then she handed him a sandwich. "You could probably leverage up on your elbow and eat this with the other hand. Right or left?"

He took the sandwich with his right hand and leaned his weight on his left elbow so that his head was raised up enough that he could chew and swallow. He glared at the woman. "Explain to me what this is."

She stared right back. "You first."

Holden didn't say anything. He ate the sandwich. When she handed him the apple, he ate that in silence too.

He could make up a story about just happening to be in the neighborhood. Reece had used being a wildlife photographer as his cover on his last assignment. Holden could do the same, but he didn't have a camera to back up that claim.

"What do you think this is?" he asked, handing her the apple core.

She took it then handed him the bag of crackers. "What do *you* think it is?"

He wasn't going to get anywhere with her. Still, he couldn't seem to make himself create an elaborate story. His brain was still too fuzzy. Or maybe he just didn't understand enough about her to make up a good story that she'd fall for. He didn't know, but his usual quick thinking was not working for him.

He'd break out tonight, get out of here and then…

And then what? Fail your mission? No. Failure wasn't an option. Still, he wasn't convinced this woman was the hit man. But that didn't mean she didn't know something about who the hit man was. He hadn't seen anyone else, but that didn't mean she wasn't working for someone. Or maybe the daughter of a man who killed people for a living.

It was possible. A lot was possible.

She switched out the empty plastic bag for the bottle of water in more silence. She petted the dog that had followed her in while she waited for him to finish. Sometimes she looked out the door and into the night.

She seemed…wistful. Quiet. *Sad*, a little voice inside him whispered, as if there was any reason to feel empathy for this woman he didn't know, who might just be sad because it was her job to kill him.

When he finished the water, he handed her the empty bottle. "You know, you're going to have to let me have a bathroom break at some point."

She seemed to consider this. "I suppose you're right." She eyed the chains and the bed. "Well, no time like the present."

She popped her head under the bottom of the bed, and something clanked. She did the same at the top.

"Go on, then."

He sat up, surprised it had been that easy. Then he realized that though his feet were no longer chained to the bed, they were still chained together. With only enough give to do a slow, clumsy shuffle step toward the door.

His hands were still handcuffed, but the chain between cuffs was long enough he had decent reach. He couldn't make a run for it, but he could grab her. Threaten her. There were a lot of things he could do.

She led him outside, the pace slow and wobbly. She made a hand-waving gesture in the dark. "The animals all go out here. Don't know why you can't."

"A little privacy?"

She made a harrumphing sound. "Fine. But I'm just a few steps away in the barn. You try to run for it, you'll be sorry."

"Fine," he muttered, waiting until he heard her footsteps retreat to take care of business.

Once done, he took a few steps back toward the door, but he looked around as he moved. It was pitch-black. Country dark. Insects buzzed and animals rustled about, but it was mostly quiet. He turned in a slow circle, testing the bonds of the chains on his feet, trying to get an idea of his surroundings.

Behind him, there was a building. It was little more than a dark shadow, but one of the windows had a light on that glowed. Not a barn, but a house. It looked downright homey and cozy.

And you're chained at the wrists and ankles in this homey, cozy loony bin.

She marched out of the barn, carrying the lantern. "All right. You've had your time. Come on now. Dawn comes early."

He stood where he was. She rolled her eyes in the flickering light of the lantern. She marched over to him, and he assumed she was going to grab his chain and lead him back into the barn.

He didn't let her. He managed to grab her wrist, holding her in place. "Tell me who you are and what this is," he demanded. If she was a man, he would have bent back her hand or done something to bring her to her knees.

But she was a woman, and he'd made a promise to himself a long time ago never to hurt a woman. Even if it ended badly for him in the process.

"Don't test me, Holden. It won't end well for you." She jerked her wrist out of his grasp.

He could have held on tighter, but it was the cold look in her eye, like she'd had back at the post office, that had him letting her go.

He shouldn't be fooled by her sweet demeanor. There was something under the surface with this woman.

With no warning, she pushed him over, and he couldn't maintain his balance because of the tight cuffs around his ankles. He fell awkwardly and hard on the ground, and it jarred the pain in his head so badly he groaned.

A few clanking sounds later, he realized she'd chained him to the door handle of the barn. Outside in the dark.

Then she sailed away, toward the lighted window, a dog following her like a wagging shadow in the lantern light.

Holden stared after her. His hands were chained at an awkward angle, but she hadn't chained his ankles to anything, which would make this slightly easier to get out of than the bed had been.

Maybe.

She'd told him not to test her, but of course he was going to test her. He just now realized he was going to have to be very careful not to underestimate her.

Chapter Four

Willa paced her room. She was angry. He'd grabbed her. He'd tried to intimidate her. Wearing chains! That she'd put there! It made her darn near vibrate with rage. He'd tricked her and then tried to...

What? Free himself?

She let out an annoyed huff. Jim gave her a side-eyed look from where he was curled up on his dog bed.

Worse than being angry, she felt guilty. Not just for chaining him up and taking care of the intruder the only way she knew how, but because she'd let her temper take over. Her parents had always told her that's when you made mistakes. When you let your emotions get the better of you.

That was why she hadn't followed in their footsteps. She rather liked being able to have an emotional response to things. She *wanted* to be angry, or afraid, or guilty and not have to think through every possible outcome of every possible decision she made by shoving those feelings away.

She *wanted* to be angry and not worry anger had led her into a mistake. She wanted to feel guilty, darn it. It wasn't normal to treat people like this. It wasn't normal she had to be alone. None of this was *normal*, and that wasn't her fault. It was the curse her parents had put on her simply by bringing her into this world.

She flopped onto her bed. Pam let out an aggrieved meow and moved farther up on the bed. It wasn't fair to blame them. They'd tried to get out. They'd only wanted a normal life too. She was their normal life.

But it hadn't worked.

Now there was a man chained to her barn door. She didn't know what he was after. Or why. She only knew it had to connect to her parents. She'd certainly never done anything remarkable enough to get herself a stalker.

It was summer, so she could certainly leave Holden outside overnight and he wouldn't freeze to death. He'd be fine. Even with the head injury.

Which shouldn't matter. He was here to hurt her. No matter what feelings she entertained, she had to remember that.

Holden. Was that his real name? He was probably a fluid liar. Assassins and kidnappers usually were. But usually they chose names like Bob or Pete. Not *Holden*.

Willa shook her head and got back to her feet. She would deal with him in the morning. She'd deal with everything in the morning. Hopefully her parents would get her email by then and have a plan in place.

She got ready for bed. She would sleep. She would sleep *soundly*, because she had nothing to feel guilty about. Her doors were locked. Her prisoner was locked up. There was nothing to be afraid of.

She knew she should go get the gun she kept in the kitchen cabinet. Mom and Dad always insisted she keep more than one gun, and to always have it within reach, but she hated having a deadly weapon in her room. It felt so grim.

She crawled into bed, determined to live her life on her terms. Let her parents handle their own problems. She'd gotten a message to them. Or at least tried. They didn't always get the coded emails in a timely manner.

She blew out a breath and resolutely closed her eyes. She was going to go to sleep. She was going to live her life and let her parents deal with the effects of theirs. End. Of. Story.

She lay there, repeating that to herself, as her body refused to relax and sleep. Because no matter what she told herself, reality didn't have to follow reason. Or what *she* wanted.

She wasn't sure how long she lay there, nerves taut and unable to sleep. But she wouldn't give up. Eventually exhaustion would win. *Please.*

Jim let out a low growl and got to his feet from where he'd been sleeping. His body quivered in concentration, that low growl continuing as he began to pad toward the door.

Fear shuddered through Willa. Even though Jim occasionally barked at some wild animal outside, this was different. No wild rush to go downstairs and outside. A careful, menacing growl.

What with everything that was going on, she couldn't ignore it probably *was* different.

She didn't curse her parents, or her lot in life. There was no point. She got back out of bed.

"Stay," she ordered the dog. She grabbed the first weapon she could find, the fire poker that hung by the fireplace in her room—both that acted more as decoration than were actually used functionally.

Jim whined as she walked past him. Willa gave him a sharp look. "Stay," she repeated. She wouldn't have any of her animals getting caught in the crossfire of this mess. No. She would handle it.

She wanted the independent life. She had to handle it when the danger of her parents' life spilled over into hers. That was just…it. She didn't have a choice in that. She only had a choice in how she responded.

She crept down the hall and paused at the top of the stairs. She listened intently. She could still hear Jim growling from her room. She heard the normal creaks and groans of the old house settling.

Then another creak that sounded much more like a footstep on a loose board than the others. Faint but unmistakable.

Willa took a deep breath. Her options were to go lock herself in her room and hope for the best. Call the police—something her parents would be *really* mad about. Or try to handle the intruder herself.

With a fire poker? Well, she could try to get to

her gun. The stairs led her down to the living room. She'd have to creep around through the TV room, the bathroom hallway and then to the kitchen to get there. All without accidentally running into the intruder or giving herself away.

Still, it was the best option in her mind. So she crept down the stairs. The house was dark, and though her eyes adjusted, there was no way to tell if the shadows were human beings, animals or simply her eyes playing tricks on her.

She made it to the bottom of the stairs, where she paused and listened. Nothing. Not a hint of someone moving or even breathing.

She crept forward, moving by memory and feel through the living room and TV room toward the kitchen. After making it through each room, she paused. Listened. Then moved forward again.

She finally made it to the kitchen, but even without pausing, she knew the intruder was in here. There wasn't the noise of breathing, or the sounds of footsteps, it was just a…feeling. Of not being alone.

She wouldn't be able to get her gun. Not by creeping around. She'd likely bump into the intruder, and that wouldn't be any good. She'd rather fight for her life face-to-face, in the light. So, she'd have to use the element of surprise and hope for the best. She squared her shoulders and felt around on the wall until she found the switch.

On an inner count of three, she flipped the switch on, fire poker at the ready.

Holden was standing in her kitchen, much closer to her than she'd imagined the intruder would be. How could he be within reach and she hadn't heard him?

He didn't even wince at the sudden light, though he did pull a face. "Good God," he said, pointing a gun at the bunny-shaped door stopper on the ground next to the back door. "What *is* that?"

Willa didn't bother to answer him. She swung the fire poker at him. She knew she should aim for his face or his crotch, but she couldn't quite bring herself to. So she hit the arm with the gun instead, hoping she could get him to drop it.

He barely flinched, so she raised the poker again and whacked his shoulder as hard as she could.

"Hey! Would you stop that?"

"No! You have a gun," she said, bringing the poker back so she could swing it again.

"Yeah, well, I'm not going to shoot you," he said, lowering his arm with the gun, and holding his other hand out as if it would stop another swing of the poker. "At least I won't if you stop whacking me with a… What even is that? A fire poker?"

"Yes."

"Let me guess. From 1875," he said dryly.

She looked at the slim metal object in her hand. "Well, I don't really know. It came with the house. 1875 seems unlike— Why are we discussing fire pokers?" she demanded, pointing it at him as if she could use it like a sword.

But Holden shook his head as he looked around

the kitchen. He frowned at the ceramic bear family lined up on the windowsill. "Why is this place some sort of animal menagerie of horrors?"

"Why do you have a gun?" she demanded, still waving the poker in his direction.

He looked back at her and the poker. "Why don't you?"

"Why do you ask so many questions?"

"Why do *you*?"

Willa huffed out a breath. "How did you get out of the chains?"

He grinned at her, and she knew her parents would find a million faults with how she was handling this, but chief among them would be that she was mesmerized by that grin for a second.

"Magic," he offered.

She was charmed, and that was all wrong. He had a *gun*. He was creeping around her house in the middle of the night. He'd escaped the chains she'd put on him, and not by *magic*.

"What are you doing sneaking around my house with a gun if you're not going to shoot me?"

"Trying to figure out who you are."

She frowned. If he didn't know who she was, why was he here? What was he doing? Or was he just looking for confirmation for what he already suspected? Maybe her parents not being here had thrown him off. Maybe he was looking for them, not her.

Either way, he was a threat. So she should absolutely not set down the poker. She shouldn't trust him not to shoot her.

She sighed heavily and did both. "Do you want some tea?"

Tea. She set down the weapon and offered him…tea.

"No. No, thank you." Holden shook his head at himself. Why was he being *polite?*

She shrugged. "I'm going to make some tea." She crossed over to a cabinet. She was in her pajamas. A cozy sweatshirt and shapeless sweatpants with thick socks on her feet. No wonder—it was colder in here than it was out in the dark night air. Her hair was still in the pigtail braids, and her face was as fresh as it had been before.

She didn't seem…fazed by any of this. When she opened the cabinet, he immediately saw the gun sitting there.

He adjusted his grip on his own, but she didn't grab it. She shoved it aside and pulled a tea bag out of the cabinet.

This was no cold-blooded assassin. It just didn't make any sense. He knew he could be fooled. A man would end up dead if he believed he could never be fooled.

But there was also something to be said for gut feelings. Maybe he didn't know what or who she *was*, but it wasn't a killer.

She moved around the kitchen. She pulled out a mug in the shape of an elephant, the trunk acting as the handle. It matched the teapot, which had what appeared to be a scene from *The Jungle Book* painted on it. Seriously, what alternate dimension had he fallen into?

"Where'd you get the gun?" she asked conversationally as she made the tea.

"I went back to my car." Once he'd gotten himself out of the chains, he'd made quick work of figuring out how to get back to his car. He'd seen her truck parked, then followed the gravel road behind it. A few dogs had happily trailed after him, not a one of them barking in alarm. He'd found his car, gotten his gun and his phone, but left the rest. He'd been able tell someone had gone through his stuff. He could only assume it was Willa.

She hadn't taken his gun, or his phone, or anything that was of use to him. He shook his head. He should have taken off. He should have called in to North Star instead of sending the quick message that he was okay and would have a more detailed report tomorrow.

He should accept she wasn't the person he was after and get back to the task at hand, but something about this woman…

"Why were you at that PO box this afternoon?" He had no doubt she'd answer his question with another question, but he couldn't seem to stop himself from asking them. Couldn't seem to stop himself from giving away parts of what he was doing.

She paused in her tea preparations. "It's my PO box," she said. Unconvincingly.

"No, it's not. I asked about it. Specifically. Who rented out number ten. The answer was no one."

"They aren't allowed to give you names," she said,

her back still to him as she poured hot water over her tea bag. Her movements were precise, and if he hadn't been looking for it, he might have missed the slight tremor in her fingers as she put the pot back on the stove.

"No, but they can tell me if a box is rented or not. Number ten is not rented. But I get the funny feeling you're not the person who picked up the package of illegal ammunition."

She turned to face him, eyebrows drawn together in confusion. "Illegal ammunition. What would I do with illegal ammunition?"

"That is the question."

"I..." She chewed on her lip. "I didn't get any ammunition from the box. Ever. I do sometimes use it, without it being rented to me. But I can't tell you why or for what. No, I suppose that isn't true. I *won't* tell you that."

"I could help you if you would."

She stared at him for a moment. An earnest look in those haunting green eyes. Damn it, he did not have time to be haunted.

"I don't need any help," she said at length. "Unless it means getting you out of my hair, of course."

"You're the one who chained me to a bed in your barn."

"You're the one who followed me home."

She was infuriating. Holden scrubbed a hand over his face. If she was of no danger to him, he supposed it wouldn't hurt to give her a little information. But it galled that she wasn't giving him any first. Usually he could charm, demand or threaten anything he wanted out of people.

Willa just looked at him blandly and boiled the water for her tea, answering any question he had with one of her own.

But she could have killed him. She could have fought him. She could have done a lot of things, and aside from trying to beat him with an ineffectual fire poker and chaining him to the bed and then the door, she'd bandaged his wounds, fed him and offered him tea.

Tea.

"I'm not here by accident," Holden said, gritting his teeth against the frustration he felt. "I'm here because of that PO box. It's connected to something. Something dangerous. Now, maybe you're not, but you using it is a heck of a coincidence for me to ignore."

She stood there, leaning back against the counter, and though her eyes were on his, he could tell she was somewhere else. Thinking things through. Trying to decide what to tell him.

Pressuring her wouldn't get what he wanted. He wasn't sure patience would, either, but he thought it was the better option at the moment.

"Tell me who you are, what you know and what you're after, and maybe I'll consider supplying some necessary information based on that," she said. As if the demand was reasonable when he was the one in her kitchen with a gun.

"I can't do that."

She raised an eyebrow. No matter how friendly

or familiar she acted, she was not a pushover in any way, shape or form. "Can't or won't?"

Holden shrugged. "A little bit of both."

They stared at each other, at an impasse. Her green eyes were sharp and direct, and she held the ridiculous elephant cup in small hands. Freckles dotted her nose, and the pigtails and slouchy sweats gave her a childish air. But she was no child. Her look wasn't cold like it had been at the post office or outside when he'd grabbed her arm, but it was intelligent.

Whoever she was, whatever she was, it was far more complicated than Holden wanted to give her credit for.

He felt something…shift inside him. Something snapping into place he couldn't have understood if he tried.

And he most certainly didn't want to try.

"Look…"

She frowned at his forehead. "You have…" Then she lunged at him, and because it had been so unexpected and so…bizarre, he couldn't brace himself in time. He tumbled to the ground, her on top of him.

But he quickly forgot the lunge when something exploded and splintered above them. He rolled them over so he was on top of her, protecting her from what else might come.

She looked up at him, eyes wide. "Who's after you?" she asked.

It dawned on him them. Pieces clicking together. Maybe he still didn't understand who she was, or why anyone would be after a pretty woman on some isolated farm, but it was clear.

"They're not after me, Willa. They're after you."

Chapter Five

Willa pushed Holden off her—or tried. He didn't budge. Even when Jim skittered into the kitchen, whining and barking at turn. She pushed Jim away from her face, where he was enthusiastically licking her, then tried to push Holden off her again. "That's ridiculous. No one is after me."

Which, of course, wasn't necessarily true. Someone could be after her. To be honest, she'd always expected kidnapping over murder. After all, she was more use to anyone who wanted to get something out of her parents if she was alive.

Unless someone wanted to punish her parents. A possibility, but that meant someone had to know who her parents were, then trace them to her.

Her parents had given her a yellow warning, though. It wasn't a red, but it was a warning nonetheless. To be careful. To be watchful.

Someone had shot at them. But the red dot had been on Holden, not her. "The red dot sight was on your forehead, not mine."

"That you saw," he returned. He was looking

around the kitchen, studying doors and windows. Jim had a similarly alert air about him, but the strangest thing occurred to Willa

Jim hadn't so much as growled at Holden. He'd rushed into the room, licked her face, and now sat in quivering alertness as if awaiting orders.

"We have to get out of here," Holden said. He moved off her but immediately grabbed her arm. "Keep low as possible." He started to drag her toward the TV room. She tried to shake his grip off her arm.

"You're going the wrong way."

"We're not going out the front door," he said, flicking a glance at the bunny door stopper.

"Of course not. That's the back door."

"That doesn't change my answer."

"Fine. You stay here in this drafty old house, and I'll go to my lockable-from-the-inside storm shelter."

He muttered something she couldn't quite make out. "What kind of lock?"

"One even you couldn't get out of, I promise you that. Just follow me." She led him to the back door. Jim whined behind her. "It's all right," she said soothingly to the dog. She kept low and reached up to turn the knob, but it was Holden who eased the door open.

He was different now. Sharper. *Deadly.* She had no doubt he would take down anything in his way. It gave her a cold chill, but as he eased the storm door open and held out his hand for her to take, she took it. She couldn't seem to help herself from believing he was the good guy.

They slid into the dark night. She inched forward, still crouched low. They didn't speak. They just moved, Willa leading him down the porch stairs then across the yard. Jim followed behind without making a sound.

Willa had learned the hard way her dogs couldn't wear tags like normal dogs. Because nothing in her life was *normal*, and tags clanked together when a dog walked.

She entered the barn—the one where many of her animals lived, not the one where she'd chained up Holden—Holden and Jim behind her. She moved through the soft hay and tried not to think too much about who was out there and shooting at them.

One step at a time. First they had to get to safety.

She went to the very last stall. "Hi, Creed," she murmured as the sleepy goat clopped over to her. She gave his head a pat but moved to the back of his stall, grabbing the broom. As quietly as she could, she swept the hay out of the way of the door. There was no way to see it in the dark, but she knew where it was, knew where to feel around on the ground for the latch.

She pulled on the latch, and the heavy door groaned and creaked open. "Hurry," she whispered to Holden. She went into the opening first, dangling her legs until she could get her feet on the rungs of the rope ladder that would take her down into the dark space.

Once they were in with the door closed, even in daylight, anyone would be hard-pressed to find the hidden door. Creed would kick around the hay, obscuring any hints of where they'd gone.

She hoped

"What the hell," Holden muttered from above, but he followed her down the ladder into the space below.

Willa felt a pang that there was no way to get Jim down here with them, but he'd eventually go off and find a bed with the other dogs. She had more dog houses than dogs scattered about the property, and even though Jim was mainly a house dog, he knew how to hang with the outside dogs.

She reached solid ground and hopped off the rope. A few seconds later, Holden followed suit.

"I closed the door behind me but couldn't feel a lock."

Willa shook her head. "It locks from down here." She called it a cellar, but it was more of a safe house. There were provisions and tunnels out, if they needed out. Her parents had *insisted* on this when she'd informed them she wanted a place of her own. Willa had let them build in whatever security measures they'd wanted. She'd felt like she was humoring them.

Apparently not.

She brought the generator to life, flipped on the lights, then booted up the computer that would allow her to lock the door—and any other door on the property she wanted.

"What…is this?" Holden said, sounding somewhere between bewildered and awed.

Willa looked around the spacious room. It had most of the comforts of home, including actual walls over the metal casing. There was a little kitchenette on one side. Cots that weren't too uncomfortable on the other. A door that led to a bathroom with all the necessary indoor plumbing. She could live down here for a year and never have to go aboveground.

A depressing thought.

"Where do these doors go?"

"Different places," Willa said, suddenly feeling tired. Not with being shot at. She'd lived with her parents too long to be surprised or overly upset by that. She was tired of having to endure her parents' lifestyle on her own.

Except... She studied Holden. She supposed she wasn't alone, but this stranger wasn't exactly the biggest comfort. Still, better than alone, she supposed.

With the computer humming, she armed the lock and engaged the video feed. Once her parents got her message, they'd be able to see the feed, too, and determine if they needed to come help. Or send help.

Oh, she really hoped they didn't send help.

"Who *are* you?" Holden asked, that baffled tone back in his voice, but with none of the irritated exasperation he'd had over her ceramic bears.

"How many times are you going to ask me that?" she wondered, tapping a few more security measures to life.

"How many times are you going to answer that with a question of your own?"

She shrugged negligently. When she turned to face him, his expression was...new. Hard. Furious. He hadn't had that look on his face even when she'd offered him a chained dinner earlier. Even when he'd tried to threaten her.

This look was devoid of all confusion. All kindness. It sent a cold shudder of fear down her spine, but she fought to keep her expression neutral, even if on the inside she was scared.

Never show an enemy your weakness, sweetheart. Always be on guard.

Her father's voice smothered some of the fear. Because it just made her feel sad. It made her think of the things she hadn't shouted at her father that she'd wanted to. *I don't want enemies! I don't want to be on guard! I just want to be normal.*

"You have to tell me," Holden said, his voice like ice as he adjusted the grip of his gun in his hand. "I have to know what's going on."

The fear subsided more. It was hard to be scared when you were just exhausted. "Or what? You're going to shoot me?"

HOLDEN LOOKED DOWN at the gun in his hand that she'd nodded to. It was pointed at the floor, but he didn't blame her for the question. He was pissed and gripping the weapon a little too tightly.

He purposefully loosened his grasp, rolled his shoulders and tried to get a leash on his temper. It wasn't her fault this had spiraled out of his control. He'd made some clear missteps here. From letting himself get injured to not leaving when he'd had the chance.

Taking out his frustration over that on her wouldn't

get them anywhere. The problem was he didn't know what would. He'd never been in a situation like this—where the person he was trying to help had so many secrets he didn't know how to even begin to untangle them.

And worse, she didn't seem like the type of woman who had secrets. He kept forgetting himself because she seemed…

She'd hit him with a fire poker. She surrounded herself with animals—real and fake—at every turn. She lived in a crumbling old farmhouse and wore slouchy sweats and looked pretty as a picture.

Now they were in some high-tech cellar hiding out from the shooter. "How does a solitary farm girl who defends herself with a fire poker have all this hidden underground?"

"I'm not a girl," she muttered. "I'm a grown woman. And none of that matters."

"How exactly does it not matter when someone is trying to kill you?"

"*You* were the target," she returned.

"I'm not the target. It's impossible." He'd been sent here to save her. He'd been sent here to take the hit man out.

She gave him a haughty look and crossed her arms over her chest. "The red sight light was on you."

He opened his mouth to argue, but that was just reflex habit. Because she was right. He hadn't seen the light. She had.

And she'd tackled him to the ground. The horrifying realization that she had saved his life slammed into him all at once. He'd been so focused on her, on the house, he hadn't thought there might be someone outside. Someone targeting them. This odd little farm girl with a full-powered underground safe house had saved *his* life.

He felt oddly…weightless. Like he'd lost all tether to the ground. "You saved me."

She blinked once, then twice, as if she hadn't realized that either. "I…suppose I did."

He didn't believe he was the target, per se. He was here to stop a hit man, which meant he was likely now a target as well as the actual target. But how could *she* be one?

Yet she'd chained him to a bed. Then a door. She'd also fed him and bandaged him. When he'd broken into her house, she'd hit him with a fire poker. Then saved him from a gunshot wound.

She made no sense. *This* made no sense. But she'd saved his life. His *life*.

Maybe he had to be the one to give first. He raked a hand through his hair. Hell, he hated giving in to anything, but he'd be little more than brain-matter splatter if not for her.

Quite unfortunately, he owed her some answers. He blew out a breath, once more taking in the scene around him. He wasn't even sure North Star had anything like this in all their various hideouts scattered around Wyoming, South Dakota and Montana.

Her computer tech wasn't as fancy as Elsie's, but it had a security camera, among other things. And apparently some kind of internet connection even underground.

Holden studied the split screen. There was a feed of the interior of the barn they'd sneaked into, and what he thought might be the exterior. On the dark exterior screen, Holden couldn't make out anything, but she must have had infrared on the interior camera, because when a man crept into the barn, Holden could see him.

"Do you know him?" he asked. The resolution wasn't very good, so his face wasn't clear, but the general appearance would be something to go on if you knew someone well enough.

She squinted at the grainy man on the camera. "It's hard to tell. I don't think so."

He couldn't ignore the fact that she gave him answers on occasion. Probably more than he'd given her. *And she saved your life.*

"I work for a group."

She turned away from the computer to study him. "A group?"

"A secret group. I can't tell you everything, but I can tell you I was sent to Evening to track a hit man."

"So, he is after you."

"No," he replied, tamping down his frustration. Why was she so reluctant to believe she was the target when she had all this? "He doesn't know I'm after him. He's looking to kill someone."

There was a flicker of something in her expression, and she looked away from him. "Why?" she asked, but her voice had changed. Guarded.

"I don't know the whys. Or the whos. Or the hows. All I was given was the fact ammunition for the gun we know was sent to him was shipped here. It was my job to unearth whatever clues I could. That led me to you. You used the same PO box."

"It was a coincidence."

"I might have believed that if I weren't standing in the middle of all this." He swept out an arm to encompass the entire room. "This isn't the kind of thing people have if there isn't the potential they'll be threatened at some point."

"Do I really seem like the kind of person who'd be threatened?" she asked, lifting her chin.

"No, you don't. But the circumstances undermine everything you *seem*, Willa."

She didn't say anything to that. She watched the man on the screen. There was no recognition in her gaze, and the line between her eyebrows pointed to a woman who was utterly baffled.

But she had all this. What could it mean? She seemed alone here, but that didn't mean she *was* alone. There were times at North Star headquarters when only Betty and Elsie were around, two young women who had impressive skills but weren't trained operatives. Could he have stumbled upon a similar group, with a woman who just wasn't a field operative?

Or a woman who was connected to someone like him. A woman who could be a threat because of what she'd mean to someone else. "It's not you. It's someone you're connected to."

She whipped her head around to look at him, which was how he knew he hit the mark.

"What? Husband? Boyfriend?" He ignored the odd tight feeling in his chest at trying to imagine what kind of man would leave her here and unprotected.

She snorted. "Honestly."

"A family member, then? Someone who could be gotten to through you. Or someone who pissed off the wrong guys. But why would anyone leave you behind, on your own?"

Her spine had stiffened, and her gaze was intent on the screen. But Holden didn't think she really saw anything. She was just trying to keep her gaze off him and her feelings under wraps.

But he'd hit a sore spot, or she wouldn't be ramrod straight and silent. Not Willa.

"I'd certainly have some resentment if I was left helpless on my own."

"I'm not helpless, and I was hardly left alone. You have no idea how hard I had to work to be independent. To convince them I could…" She trailed off and closed her eyes in disgust.

She'd given away a lot more than she'd planned, that much was clear. "Them. Parents. Who are your parents, Willa?"

"Who's your *group*, Holden?" she shot back.

He might have been frustrated to have questions answered with questions again, but she stood, anger sparking off her, and it left him speechless.

Her eyes flashed, she advanced on him, and if it

hadn't been for his excessive training, he might have actually retreated out of sheer surprise.

"I'm not the only one who can guess things. Who can use what you've said and haven't said against you." She poked him in the chest.

He raised a warning eyebrow, but her anger was clearly impeding her judgment completely. "This group of yours," she said, disgust dripping off every word. "You set off to do good things, but under some kind of mask so you don't have to follow laws." She poked him again.

This time he grabbed her wrist. "Watch it."

She wrenched her hand out of his grasp. "Oh, I'll watch it." She flung her arms in the air. "You're so derisive of them leaving me alone, but you must not have anyone in your life. That's it, isn't it? You had no one in your life so you joined some vigilante group to feel fulfilled. Ignore laws, ignore rules and pretend to be Superman. Prance around feeling important because you risk your life you clearly don't care all that much about. Well, you must not have anyone you love. Your parents must be dead and you must not have any siblings or grandparents or anyone you care about. Or maybe more important, no one who cares about you."

It shouldn't have hurt. Why should the truth, more or less, hurt? But he found himself wanting to rub his heart—not where she'd poked, but where it beat despite the ache inside. "Well, Willa, direct hit."

Chapter Six

Holden betrayed no emotion on his face, and yet it felt like the entire space around them was filled with an aching, painful throb of hurt.

It was all her fault. She'd only been so angry he'd seen right through her. Angry that she'd betrayed her parents in a way. No one was ever supposed to know, and yet…

There was no way to hide it from Holden. Not when they were being shot at. She believed his story. Clearly there was a hit man. What didn't add up to her way of thinking was why he'd shot at Holden first.

If the hit man was meant to kill her, it was punishment for her parents. A message or something. *Yes, we know who your daughter is. Yes, we'll kill anyone you've ever loved.*

She fought off the shudder of fear. She was inside and safe. He was out there.

She had a strange man to deal with in here. One who wasn't going to kill her. More than likely anyway.

"I mean, you got a few key things wrong," Holden said flippantly, with a careless shrug.

He was a very good actor, and yet she found she didn't believe the flippant or careless remarks. Maybe she couldn't see evidence of it, but she could *feel* his hurt.

"The parents are dead, sure. By the time I was sixteen. I had quite a few brothers and sisters, though, but the funny thing about being an orphan is you don't often get to keep them. When you're sixteen, there's not a whole lot you can do about it. Whether you care or not."

The story broke her heart. She didn't think he meant it to. She didn't think he meant her to feel anything. But she couldn't help it. "I'm sorry."

He fixed her with a glare. "I don't know why you'd be sorry."

"Because I don't know what it's like to have brothers or sisters, but I can't imagine how hard it would be to lose them *and* parents. To be left alone."

"Oh, I wasn't alone. I was ripe pickings for the gang in the neighborhood. Vigilante group? Lady, that 'vigilante' group saved my life. And you have no idea the good we've done in the world."

He whirled away from her, shoving his hand through his hair. She could tell he didn't know why he was telling her this. He was irritated with himself.

It was foolish to sit here and think *poor boy* when he was a man with a gun, with a mission. When, if she really was the target, his job was to save her.

You saved me, he'd said. Awed and, if she wasn't totally mistaken, not quite comfortable with it.

She couldn't say she was comfortable with it either. She hadn't meant to. She'd just…acted.

"This is all irrelevant," he said, turning back around to face her, and there was a blank coldness in his expression that said loud and clear *this* conversation was over and he was in charge now.

Willa had no desire to be *in charge*. Her plan was to wait for her parents to get her message and take care of their own mess.

But she couldn't tell Holden that. He'd figured out way more on his own than her parents would be comfortable with. Then she'd lashed out like a petulant child.

And hit the mark.

He frowned at the security feed. The man was still poking around the barn. "Can you get a picture of him?" he demanded.

"Yes, but it's not going to be enough to go on."

"We'll decide if it's enough. Take the picture." He pulled his phone out of his pocket and dialed.

"Oh, you won't be able to get service down…" She trailed off as he raised an eyebrow. Apparently he had some tech of his own. He turned away from her and spoke into the phone. "Els? I'm sending you a picture of someone I want you to try to get an ID on."

Willa watched him talk to *Els*, on a phone that shouldn't have worked underground. He was still tense, focused on the mission, but there was a comfort, an understanding there. He had people he could call and work side by side with.

She had nothing.

She looked back at the computer. It was silly to feel sad, to check her email quickly, hoping for some response from her parents.

Nothing.

There was a man who wanted her dead. She should be far more worried about that than her lack of human companionship. Especially since her parents hadn't gotten her message. What if they were dealing with their own problems and her SOS never reached them?

Holden came to stand next to her, but not because he was going to talk to her or involve her. He tugged the keyboard away from her and began to tap away, listening to the woman on the phone.

She watched as he took the picture she'd taken and converted it into a file and sent it off to some unknown email address.

He made noises into the receiver, giving assent every so often. "Got it," he said into the phone as he pushed the keyboard back to her. "Keep me updated." He shoved the phone back into his pocket, then took a moment to study her.

Willa frowned at him, studying him right back. He stood awfully close, since he'd needed access to the computer she was sitting in front of. She could see the bandage she'd originally put on his head had bled through and needed changing. Still, even with the bloody head, the hours of unconsciousness earlier today, he seemed…completely strong and capable.

His blue eyes were guarded and alert. He still held the gun as if it was a part of his arm. He was tall and broad and *strong*, and it was odd that she wasn't really…afraid of him. He could be anyone. He could do anything to her.

But he hadn't. They'd saved each other instead. Because he hadn't disappeared when they'd been shot at. He'd said *we*.

When he finally spoke, his voice was devoid of any emotion or strain. It was straight detached authority.

"I've got a team coming to sweep the area."

"They might not find the guy," she pointed out.

He nodded. "If he can't find us, I imagine he'll disappear for a bit until he comes up with a new plan. Or report to a boss. Too many options, really, but we've got a slight visual. If my team doesn't get him, we'll see if we can't identify him and go from there." He nodded toward one of the cots in the opposite corner of the room. "You should get some sleep."

She glanced at the cot, then back at him. "What are you going to do?"

"Wait."

"Then I'll wait, too."

He shook his head and took a few steps away from her, though that steady blue gaze never left her. "You're just an innocent bystander in all this, Willa. Let the professionals handle it."

She'd been told that all her life. No, she hadn't wanted anything to do with her parents' lifestyle, but everyone acted like that meant she was helpless. A pawn to be moved around and protected, but not trusted. Not involved.

She'd saved *his* life, and he was dismissing her. It didn't sit right. At all. Maybe she didn't have a normal life, but that didn't mean she wouldn't fight for the right to *have* a life.

"No, I don't think I'm going to do that anymore."

HOLDEN FROWNED AT WILLA. He wouldn't say she looked fragile, exactly, but shadows were beginning to appear under her eyes. She was all she appeared. An innocent woman stuck in a bad situation through no fault of her own.

So, why wouldn't she let him handle it? "Look—"

"No. You look. I don't care who my parents are. I don't care who this hit man is. I don't care who you are." With each *I don't care*, the fury in her voice rose another octave. "It's my house. These are my animals and my responsibility. It's *my* life. I won't just go to sleep and let everyone else handle it. That's over now."

Holden wanted to sigh and rub his temples, but that would give the illusion of weakness, and he couldn't allow any of those. He was in charge here, and she had to understand that.

"Look, I don't know what your deal with your parents is, and you won't tell me, so I have to take this over and handle it. That's my assignment. Keep the target from ending up dead and take down the hit man."

"I'm not dead. Could I have been? Seems that way. But he decided to shoot you first. When I had my back to the window, he could have taken me out without you being the wiser. Until it was too late. So, explain to me why you think I'm the target?"

She made a few too many good points. "I'm not the target."

She shrugged. "As I've said more than once—you were the one with the sight on your head."

It grated that she was right. He still didn't think he was the target. That was instinct. But her point that she wasn't the target, either… Well, it wasn't completely off base. "Tell me about your parents, Willa," he said earnestly.

"I can't do that, Holden." Her response was just as earnest, and it almost seemed as if there was some apology in her gaze. He was deluding himself.

"Then you're of no help to me. Go to bed."

Her expression went mutinous. Furious. And there was something particularly warped inside him that he found that attractive. That he found her attractive under all these insane circumstances.

She stood in front of him, chin raised and eyes flashing. "Do you want to make a bet?"

"Huh?" He understood next to nothing about this woman, and he found that…a little too fascinating.

"A bet. Let's make a bet."

"What kind of bet?"

"If I can knock you down before you can knock me down, I help. If you knock me down first, I'll go sit in a corner like a child."

The cold chill of memory shuddered through him. "I don't fight women," he said flatly.

Her hands curled into fists, and she cocked her head to the side. "Then I guess I'll win."

She struck out, a decent jab. Holden dodged it.

She didn't just have good instincts—she'd been trained to fight. Each strike was precise, strong, and got her closer to landing the blow. He dodged, enough that most of the punches or elbows missed. Sometimes she'd land a glancing hit, but they didn't hurt.

Still, she didn't tire herself. She just kept moving forward, and Holden stayed on the defensive. Once he grabbed her fist to keep it from landing, but she only pivoted and swept a leg out.

He hissed out a breath when that kick landed. Hard. "Stop this."

"No," she said. Her voice was a little breathless, but she didn't stop. She kept advancing, striking out, missing, but never giving up. She made a glancing blow across his chin, which had him stepping back. But she'd maneuvered him on purpose—because he stepped on something and had to overcorrect to stop himself from tripping. Which gave her the chance to sweep out her leg and land a kick at just the right place on his knee to have his leg buckling.

He didn't *fall* to the ground but momentarily went down to his knee which, even if he'd be able to jump right back up if this was a *real* fight, was clearly a loss for him in her book.

She stood above him. Grinning. She was sweating a little and breathing hard, but her green eyes danced with mischief. "I win."

He scowled up at her. "I didn't fight back."

She shrugged. "That sounds like your problem." She held out a hand as if she was going to help him up.

A few scenarios ran through his mind at that

moment. Pulling her down and pinning her to the ground. Telling her *No, I think I won* chief among them. But his body had an odd, electrical response to that little fantasy, which meant he couldn't indulge it.

Still, he took her hand and let her help him up, even though he didn't need it. Her hand was slim and small, but callused and work-roughened. She was strong. A lithe kind of strength. Her fighting style wasn't graceful. It was principled, determined and effective.

She let go of his hand, but he found his own grip on her arm tightening. She raised an eyebrow at him. She wasn't exactly who she pretended to be. Or maybe she was. Maybe she was all the little facets of herself she'd shown. Friendly farm girl. Cold, icy operative. Strong, determined fighter. He wasn't sure he would believe all three facets in anyone else, but in Willa they somehow made sense.

"I'm not a child," she began reasonably. She tried to tug her hand out of his grasp once, but when he didn't loosen his grip she simply relaxed her hand in his. "I'm not even a liability. Just because I'm not part of this whole world doesn't mean I wasn't trained to fend for myself. My parents didn't leave me unprotected. They finally let me have my own life because I proved, over and over again, I could handle whatever threat came. And I did. *I* wasn't the one he shot at. You were. And, if I have to remind you, I saved your life."

Her discomfort with that had clearly disappeared, while his only grew. He said nothing, just stood there.

Still holding her hand in his. Why? He didn't have a clue.

"If we work together, Holden, we might be able to figure this out," she said, so earnest as she stepped toward him. So that there was maybe a foot between them at most. "But we'd have to tell each other everything, and I know we both think we can't. But I'd be willing to bend a little, if you were." Her green eyes were darker down here, or maybe she was just more serious. More…something. So many different people wrapped up into one.

And don't you recognize that deep in your soul?

He'd rather forget his soul had ever existed for the moment. So, he focused on reason and sense and the assignment. She was right, on too many counts. He didn't agree that meant he was the actual target, just that something more than just taking her out was going on.

There were things he *could* tell her, especially with North Star sending out a team he would no doubt need to rendezvous with. And if she would unbend a little to tell him what her parents were involved in, he could handle this. Really handle it.

"All right," he said after a while. "We can try it your way."

She grinned up at him, and there was a jolt that had him thinking about Reece again. Giving up everything he was all because some pretty woman had wrapped him up in her. Holden wouldn't follow that same path.

He wouldn't.

But he finally understood how easy it would be.

Chapter Seven

Willa's heart was hammering in her chest, but she didn't tug away her hand like she wanted to. Holden was playing some kind of power game, and she wouldn't let him see that it affected her—in any of the ways it affected her.

She wanted to clear her throat, but that would give her away, too. She kept the easy smile in place and tried to swallow surreptitiously. "Well, since I saved you and all, I think you should go first."

He stared at her for a very, *very* long time. She managed to keep her expression bland, her outward demeanor cool. Inside she was a riot of nerves and some other fluttery feeling she didn't want to give name to.

His eyes were *very* blue.

"I've told you most of it. My group is tasked with stopping a hit man. I can't be the target because the hit man doesn't know who I am or that I'm after him."

"How do you know?"

"Because I know."

She shook her head. "That's hardheaded. They could have found out."

"Okay, they found out I'm after them. That doesn't negate that they had a different target to begin with. One they're supposed to take out. Regardless of me."

She hated to admit it, but that was true. She could argue coincidence—after all, she hadn't gotten the ammunition in her PO box. She didn't know who these men were or whom they were after. Maybe they'd unwittingly involved her in something that had nothing to do with her?

But her parents had sent the warning message. Yellow meant to be on the lookout.

"It would help if we knew who your parents are," he said carefully. He was trying not to press. Not to demand. She'd give him credit for that. "And who they're involved with."

She blinked, realizing in a way she hadn't before that he…suspected her parents. Of being the bad guy in this scenario. "You think they're…" She trailed off. She wasn't supposed to out her parents. Ever. No matter the circumstances.

She had wanted to tell a great many people in her life who her parents were, or at the very least what they did. So they'd understand her. She'd always kept her mouth shut. Always swallowed down the truth. Because she was supposed to. For her safety, and for her parents' safety.

"You want to protect them," Holden said softly. "I understand. We always want to protect our parents, but have they protected you?"

"Yes. Always. You don't understand. You couldn't. They tried…" Willa moved away, and Holden finally let her hand go. She had to move. She had to think. She had... Oh, what she wouldn't give to have one of her animals down here to cuddle into for a minute or two.

But there was only Holden. Which meant she had to rein herself in. Figure things out. Decide what was worth telling and what wasn't. She had to use her brain. Just because she hadn't followed in her parents' footsteps didn't mean she didn't know how to figure out a difficult situation.

The facts were facts. And if she arranged them without emotion, she could put together the puzzle enough to make the next step. "My parents could be the targets. They could be the ones this hit man is supposed to kill."

"They've done things worth killing over?" he asked. Blandly enough, but the question had her temper simmering again.

She aimed a haughty look over her shoulder. "Haven't you?" she returned.

His expression didn't change much, though she could have sworn the air between them got colder. "This isn't about me."

"No, but you're in the same boat, aren't you?"

"Am I?"

Temper straining, she started pacing again. "Oh, you're more obstinate than a goat."

"I don't know what to say to that, but you're not exactly amenable yourself."

She let out a huffy breath. Of course she wasn't. Of *course* she wasn't. She didn't owe him amenability.

But she didn't see a way out of this, a way to help her parents, if she didn't offer him a glimpse into who they were. They hadn't responded to her SOS. They could be fighting off their own thing. They could be out of range. They could be oblivious.

She couldn't reach them. Not if they didn't want to be reached.

Holden had told her…next to nothing. But he'd wanted to tell her nothing, so she supposed *next to* was something. It wasn't just *his* secret he'd told her. He'd mentioned a group, talked to a woman named Els on the phone. A team was coming to look for their shooter.

"What's your last name?" she asked.

He paused, considering. Considering if he was going to tell her? Coming up with a fake name? So many things that pause could mean.

"My name is Holden Parker. I can't tell you the name of the group I work for, but we're an independent group who only takes on jobs that will help people. Yes, I've done things people would want to kill me over. Maybe it's rationalization, but I like to think that as long as I've been with this group, every thing I've done wrong has been in the name of right and protecting innocent people."

He said it all so seriously. So intently, his eyes on hers. He could have been lying, but there was such *conviction* in his voice, in his gaze.

"What about before you were with this group?" she asked, not sure why her voice came out so hushed.

"My before doesn't really matter here, Willa."

Sadly, he was right on that score. She'd wanted to know for herself, and that wasn't fair. "My parents aren't all that different. I can't tell you the group they work for, because I don't know. Before I was born, they were with the CIA. They tried to quit. They didn't want to be spies anymore. They wanted a normal life. With me. But it never worked out that way, and after years of jumping around trying to escape the demands of who and what they were, they gave up. They took jobs to do good in the world." She swallowed. "I didn't want to be a part of it, so once I was an adult and could convince them to leave me on my own, I did. They take the jobs they want, that they think will do some good. And I have nothing to do with it. Except to be their liability. Because they love me. Because I'm theirs."

Holden looked around the room they were in. "That's why you have all this?"

She nodded. "And no friends. It's why I don't talk to the post office lady. I have to be alone. Separate. So that no one can use me to get to them."

She'd always thought it would feel freeing to tell someone the truth. The real truth, but she just wanted to cry. To take it all back. Because now it was up to Holden not to use that information against her.

And once again, she didn't have any say in the matter.

SPIES.

But it wasn't that revelation that left Holden speechless. It was the sheen of tears in Willa's eyes.

It hadn't been easy for her to tell him all that. She'd probably promised to always keep it a secret. Especially if her parents were government spies.

But she'd told him.

He shouldn't feel awed or humbled by that. She'd had no choice. There was a hit man out there. If she hoped to survive, she had to trust someone.

And she really trusted you?

"If you've kept this separation, how would anyone know you're connected to them?" he asked, instead of addressing any of the emotion in the room. Because emotions didn't matter, couldn't matter, when lives were at stake.

"There are always ways to find things out, no matter how deep you bury them. This has always been possible."

"What was the consensus? You'd just be killed for their job?" He didn't know why anger spurted through him. Why he held such blame and contempt for two people he didn't know. Who were probably a lot more like him than he'd want to admit.

"It's easy to blame them, Holden. Believe me. I know. I've done it. But what were they supposed to do? See into the future and know they'd never be able to escape one job they took because they wanted to do good in the world?"

Holden didn't know what to say to that. He *wanted* to argue, but this wasn't the topic of importance right now. He had to figure out what they were going to do if the North Star team swept the area and didn't find the hit man. If Elsie couldn't get an ID.

Willa would still be in danger if they didn't take this man down. Holden's assignment was to take the man down—just as much as it was to keep the target from being killed.

"Something isn't right," Willa muttered to herself.

"Gee, you think?"

"No. More than just…someone being after me. Or you. Or…whatever is going on. Something doesn't add up. I got a message to them." Her frown deepened, and she twisted her fingers together. "I sent them an SOS, but they haven't responded. I just can't stop thinking about the fact that he could have killed me, and he didn't. Which means he wants me…not dead. Not yet. So, why?"

"Kidnapping."

"Yes. I've always been aware that could happen. Kill you. Take me. But then what? My parents warned me to be on alert, more so than usual. That's what I was getting from the PO box. A message from them. A warning. They knew something was off, but they didn't tell me to hide. They just told me to be careful."

"They thought they could take care of it?"

"Maybe. Or maybe it was only a feeling—no fact. You'd understand that, wouldn't you? Sometimes they just *feel* like something is off and they don't know why, they just know it is." She looked at him with heartbreaking eyes.

He had to stay strong against those eyes. "Yeah, I understand that."

"It feels like something is off. I know I'm no spy,

or…whatever you call yourself. But it doesn't add up. Not cleanly. And it should."

Holden tried to look at things from her perspective. Someone who'd probably known from an early age she could be a target like this. It made sense to trust her judgment on the matter.

"We've got tech on our end—bigger than what you have here. We could try to get a message to them."

She shook her head. "It's too dangerous. For them." She sucked in a breath. "They'd do anything to protect me. And have. I don't know the details, but I know they've sacrificed to keep me safe. I have to do the same for them. I just have to."

Holden didn't say what he wanted to. *But I don't have to.*

"I've done the one thing I'm allowed to do if there's an emergency."

"Do you hear yourself? *Allowed* to do." He tried to tamp down his anger over the position her parents had put her in. He knew what it was like to be naive and young and unprotected. How easy it was for so many bad things to happen. "You're a grown woman. Act like it. Make your own choices."

Her expression hardened. "Believe me. I do."

He wanted to argue some more. Or maybe just order her around so that he could do his job and stop dealing with all these conflicting emotions that had more to do with who he'd been before North Star, before the Sons. A person from a very long time ago who didn't exist anymore.

He'd left all that behind. But she'd somehow brought it all back to life inside him.

Enough.

His phone chimed, and he pulled it out to look at the message. Clean. Meet?

They'd sent Gabriel. By Holden's opinion, Gabriel would make a good replacement for Reece. He was still a little young, and Holden would give him a few more challenging missions before he actually put him in a lead position, but it was good Shay had chosen him to lead the sweep.

"I'm going up," he told Willa. "You'll stay here."

"No, I'm coming with you."

"You're staying here."

"I need to take care of my animals. I can set things up so they're okay for a few days on their own if I have to, but you have to let me do that first."

He knew he shouldn't be weak, shouldn't give in, but he also understood fully that she had all those animals and animal figurines because she couldn't have people in her life. She'd filled the void with things that couldn't be used against her or her parents.

"We can't take chances. You have to stick with me until we have a better idea of what's going on. Regardless of your animals."

"You're not my boss, Holden. I didn't ask for you or your group. This is my life you've crashed into. I don't owe you diddly squat."

Holden didn't know why that hurt. She was right. She hadn't asked for this, and technically she had very little to do with what he was here for. He was here to stop a killer—not protect Willa, but to stop the person trying to hurt her. There was a gray area there in how to do it, but his job wasn't *her*.

"Whether you asked for it or not, my assignment isn't fulfilled if you're dead. So, I'm going to ask you to do as I say. I'm going to ask you to trust me to keep you safe while we stop the man who's after you—however he's after you."

She seemed to consider that, watching him with green eyes he knew with a glaring clarity that would haunt him no matter the outcome of this mission. She closed the computer and flicked a switch that had the lights dimming and the sound of the generator going silent.

"I could trust you, Holden, but trust is a two-way street." She turned to one of the doors and flipped a combination on the lock. It creaked open, and she pulled it the rest of the way open. "If we go through here, we can get in through the house and not disturb Creed. Have your man meet us at the front door. East side of the house."

She didn't wait for him to agree. She simply slid into the dark tunnel. Holden blew out a frustrated breath and texted Gabriel. Then he followed her into the dark.

Chapter Eight

Willa half wished she could stay in the dark tunnel that would lead her into the basement of her house. Here in the dark, her life was not in danger. There was no team. Her parents were off somewhere safe.

And she didn't already trust a man who distrusted her. A man she barely knew. A man she *shouldn't* trust, because this could all be an elaborate lie.

But she couldn't work herself up to that kind of suspicion. So, she'd just have to trust him and hope for the best. Hope to hear from her parents soon.

"This is some movie-level stuff," Holden said from behind her in the tunnel. She'd unlocked the door to the basement before she'd shut down the computer in the main room so when she reached it, she only had to pull it open.

She didn't bother to respond to Holden. Maybe it was movie-level stuff. But it was also her life. The only life she'd ever known. Whatever attempt her parents had made at normal had been mostly before she'd been old enough to remember.

So, she'd grown up with security measures and over-the-top tech, all in the name of keeping her safe.

Everyone always trying to keep her safe.

She shoved away the bitterness. It didn't do her any good. She waited for Holden to follow her through the door before she closed it back up. She set the lock from the outside, then pulled the false wall in front of it.

The basement was dark, but Holden had pulled up the flashlight on his phone. He pointed it at the wall, where you could no longer tell there was a door.

"Serious movie-level stuff," he muttered. "Gabriel is waiting on the porch."

Gabriel. "Do you use real names?" Her parents didn't. Code names, usually. Even with people they worked closely with on the same mission, she didn't think they ever used their real names. Even with her, they were simply Mom and Dad.

She thought about Holden saying his parents had died when he'd been a teenager. He'd had those years of normalcy, supposedly. And still tragedy had touched his life.

None of which mattered. All that mattered was figuring out who'd shot at them. She would be part of it. She would not be hidden away like her parents always forced her to be. Not as long as they didn't respond to her message.

She would not hide in case they were in trouble. She would not *cower* just because things didn't make sense. They'd trained her to fight. Taught her to be self-sufficient.

No one would push her away from the opportunity of helping them if they were in danger.

She moved through the basement. Holden used his light to follow her, but she knew the way in the dark. When he finally responded to her question about real names, his voice was clipped. Detached.

"Yes. Most of us. For the most part, whoever we are or were disappears once we join the group. So our names are safe. Not really tied to anyone."

They used their real names. But disappeared when they joined the group. She had to assume they weren't tied to anyone because his group collected people who didn't *have* anyone. People like him who'd lost his family.

They climbed the stairs in silence, and Holden gently pulled her back before she could open the door. He slid it open himself, inch by inch, leading with his gun. He held a hand out behind him—a silent order to stay where she was until he made sure it was safe.

She frowned a little but remained where she was. Being involved, making sure her parents were okay didn't mean she had to take risks or chances. Sometimes she'd have to rely on Holden's experience.

And sometimes he'd have to rely on hers. Whether he realized it now or not.

Eventually he motioned her forward, and in silence she followed him through the house and to the front door. He shined his light on the bunny doorstop that lay askew.

"Did you move that when you broke into my house?" she asked in a whisper.

"Yeah," he replied. "What the hell are those things?"

"Doorstops. The house is old. In the spring and summer if I want the doors open, I have to use the stops."

He shook his head. "Why *rabbits*?"

"What's wrong with rabbits?"

"They're rodents, Willa."

"What's wrong with rodents?"

Holden muttered something unintelligible and eased the heavy door open. The storm door opened from the other side, and a man slid in the opening.

"Parker," he greeted Holden.

"Gabe. What have you got?"

"No sign of the shooter. Based on our scan, he acted alone. There is a problem though."

"Yeah, what's that?"

"The shells we found? They don't go in the gun we're looking for."

It was strange. Appearance-wise Holden and this Gabriel were night and day—dark and light—and yet they *felt* the same standing there. It was in the posture, or the air of power, or *something*. You knew they were trained to handle whatever came their way.

You were, too.

But one thing she'd learned—not from her parents, but from experience—was it was best when she was underestimated. So, she didn't tell them her theory. And when Gabriel and Holden went outside to "check the perimeter"—which she knew translated as "have a talk without the woman"—Willa got to a little work of her own.

"WHERE'D SHE COME FROM?" Gabriel wanted to know as they walked the perimeter of the house. Much as Holden trusted Gabriel and the other team members, there were some things he wanted to see for himself. Like where the shells had been. Like the shells themselves.

"What do you mean?" Holden asked, searching the dark for some sign of…something. Who shot at someone, missed and then just disappeared?

It didn't add up. Which Willa had pointed out very astutely.

"Nice-looking."

Holden straightened like a shot. Based on the way the other man's eyes widened, he assumed his face was arranged in a way that screamed *murder*. He tried to school it into something softer. The sharp disapproval of a teacher, rather than…wanting to strangle him with his bare hands.

"She's a victim in a situation we're trying to mitigate, Saunders."

"I didn't say we weren't," he returned, but the words were careful. Measured. "Just commentary."

"Commentary is best kept to yourself unless it's relevant to the assignment."

"Yes, sir."

There was some sarcasm in the *sir*, but that didn't bother Holden any. Made him feel a *little* old, when he wasn't. Well, maybe by North Star standards he was. Especially now that Reece was gone. Wasn't everyone but Shay and Betty younger than him?

Holden grimaced. He didn't want to be *old*, even if it was just in this small microcosm of people.

But he was the leader, and he had assignments to lead. "I want the shells back at headquarters for tests. You can send someone else. I want you to stay close as secondary."

Gabriel nodded. He stopped at a rock a few yards from the house. "This is where I found the shells."

Holden studied the area. He'd want to look again in the daylight instead of the two narrow beams of light from their phones. But this would be a good vantage point. Still, how had Holden not sensed something was wrong? Why hadn't any of her dogs?

Granted, they didn't really bark or growl at him. Wouldn't the point of having all those animals around be for them to act as some kind of protective element? Or at least an early alarm?

So many things that didn't fully add up. He looked back at the house. Willa had a light on and was in the kitchen. Probably cleaning up the shattered glass.

"We need the bullet too," he said, watching the shadow of her movements. She'd told him things, and yet he knew she'd kept things from him, too. Probably always would. His job was to protect her, but she'd protect her parents.

He wanted to blame her for that, but it was hard to find the frustration. If his parents were alive, he'd do everything in his power to protect them too.

"Something doesn't add up here," Gabriel said, his voice low and quiet in the dark of night.

"No, it doesn't." Holden crouched by the rock, tried

to figure the angle of the shooter. Tried not to think about how he should have been more careful.

Eventually he stood. "Do another check. Not as wide, but even more thorough. I'll get the bullet and meet you back out here."

"Afraid to let me inside because I've got eyes in my head?"

Holden didn't give Gabriel a look. He would have said the same thing once upon a time. Hell, if Sabrina was leading this and he was on secondary, he would have said the same to her. The fact it *annoyed* him was neither here nor there.

So, he said nothing at all. He strode for the house and trusted Gabriel to do his job. He went in through the front door, studying the house with new eyes. When he'd first sneaked in, he'd been looking for signs of who Willa really was. Now he was looking for signs of weakness.

She had that whole safe house underground setup and she lived in this rickety old farm house like she didn't have a fear in the world. Where she tried to live a normal life, with only animals for companionship.

He could not let that affect him. Sympathy, empathy, they weren't the enemy, but they could make it harder to do what had to be done. Much as he felt his new mission was to protect Willa, he couldn't trust her one hundred percent. She still had secrets.

Soundlessly, he made his way to the kitchen. He stood in the shadows, just out of sight, watching her sweep up glass. She talked the entire time. To a dog and a cat who sat obediently away from the glass.

"Windows can be replaced," she was saying. "Any *thing* can be replaced." She sighed, resting on her haunches—broom in one hand, dustpan in the other. She looked at her animals. "I don't know how I'm going to protect you guys though."

"We'll figure out something."

She jerked in surprise, but she didn't screech or fall over. She simply eyed him warily. "Will *we* now?"

"Much like you, they're innocent bystanders."

She sighed and got to her feet, dumping the dustpan's contents into a paper bag. The glass clinked together, and she looked up at the window that had exploded. She'd taped cardboard over the opening.

"Innocent bystander. I don't feel like that. I feel like a pawn."

Since that's essentially what she was, he chose to change the subject. "Do you have anything I could dig the bullet out of the wall with?"

She turned and studied the wall where there was a hole. It didn't bother Holden that it could have been his head that bullet had been lodged into. He'd been shot at too many times to count. He had a healthy grip on the idea of mortality.

But Willa had gone a little pale as she studied the wall. He wondered how deeply she'd considered her own. Likely more than the average woman, but that didn't mean some people ever got comfortable with it.

She turned away and opened a drawer. She pawed around in what appeared to be a collection of junk— rubber bands and random screws, cords and pieces of paper, then pulled out a pair of needle-nosed pliers.

She handed him the tool, and he worked to get the bullet out of the wall with minimal damage to the wall, but either age or damage made much of the drywall and plaster crumble away as he dug around for the bullet.

Much like the shells, the bullet didn't match the ammunition for the high-powered gun they knew about. Still a deadly bullet and weapon, but Holden had to wonder why a hit man who'd been sent a specific weapon would then use a different one.

The only reason he could think of was that Willa wasn't the target. Not specifically. He didn't want to worry her, but she had a connection to two people hooked up with government missions and danger.

"Willa…" He sighed. "Do you know where your parents are?"

Her expression didn't change. There was no shock or worry or surprise. Because clearly she'd already come to the same conclusion he had. "I don't know. They're not answering my messages." Willa looked back at the window and hugged her arms around herself. "You think they're the actual target."

There was no getting around it. "Yes."

When she looked back at him, her eyes were direct, no sign of tears. Her expression was grim, but not afraid. "I do too. Which means you have to help me find them."

Chapter Nine

Holden's mouth moved into a frown. A disapproving one. She knew it would be difficult, but she had to convince him to let her be part of his assignment. She couldn't sit back while her parents were in specific danger.

She'd done it her whole life. Let them be in danger. Just...*hoped* they'd be okay and she wouldn't be left helpless and alone. But what if they needed her now? What if that's why they hadn't responded to her help message? What if they *couldn't*? Could she really just sit around and wait for news they were dead?

No, she couldn't.

This was different from anything that had come before because they weren't communicating with her. Because Willa herself had been shot at, not just threatened. Besides, in this moment she had... Well, Holden wouldn't see himself as her partner, but they *could* act as partners. For this. She just needed to be a part of it.

She wished her doubts about Holden were more pronounced. They *should* be. Intellectually she knew she'd already given too much, trusted too much. But when push came to shove, she couldn't seem to help it.

And he hadn't tried to hurt her, had he?

"My assignment is to stop the hit man, Willa. It's what I'll do. If your parents are the target, I'll do everything in my power to protect them."

"You need my help."

He dropped the bullet into a bag. He'd send it back to his group and hope to get some information from the study of it, if she had to guess.

"You won't be left unprotected, Willa. Even if he shot at me, clearly you're a target in all this."

"I'm not worried about me. I'm worried about them. You have to let me help."

"Help what?"

"Help with your assignment. You don't know my parents. You don't know who they are or what they look like."

"I don't know the hit man either. I'll find both. It's my job to find both. Whether you want to believe it or not, I'm very good at my job."

Oh, she *wanted* to believe it, but that didn't make it possible for her to sit on the sidelines. Not this time. Not until she heard from her parents directly. "It'd be easier with my help."

"I don't see how."

"Do you want me to prove I can shoot a gun? That I can sneak around unheard? Do you want me to prove everything they taught me, because I can. I will."

"It's not that I doubt your…capabilities."

But he did. Of course he did. He looked at her and

saw a weak, silly woman surrounded by animals. No matter how much she explained to him how she'd been trained to protect herself, he wouldn't believe it. She could probably *prove* it and he wouldn't believe it.

Because he didn't want to. Didn't have to.

"Fine." And it was fine. She wasn't tied to him. She didn't need him. She had her own two feet. Her own mind. Her own choices. "I'll go after them on my own."

"Not an option," he said, his voice cold and authoritative.

Which stirred the anger she was using to cover up her paralyzing fear. "So funny—I don't remember consenting to let you boss me around or tell me what I can't do."

He groaned out loud. "Willa. Just...hit pause, okay? It's the middle of the night. You're tired. You've been shot at. Let's just go to sleep. We'll talk about it in the morning."

"Oh, *we're* going to go to sleep?"

His expression was bland. "Sure."

"For some kind of spy, you're a terrible liar."

"I'm not a spy, and I'm not *lying*. I'm trying to do my job and you're getting in the way. How are you going to help me? I know what I'm doing. I'm *trained* in what I'm doing. You're a farmer."

"I know their habits. How they operate. I may not know where they are, but I can tell you things about their past missions that might give you an idea where to start. Yes, you have the whole whatever-you-are-that-isn't-a-spy thing down, but I know *them*. If we work together, we can save them faster. I'm sure of it."

The back door swung open. Willa jumped, though she stopped a surprised shriek from exiting her mouth. A woman stood there, and Holden immediately relaxed his hand on his weapon. Though he was clearly surprised by the woman's appearance.

"Shay."

Willa blinked at the woman. She was tall and, well, very pretty. Her hair was blond, her eyes were blue, and Willa figured if she wasn't dressed head to foot in tactical gear, you might even be convinced she looked elegant.

But she *was* in tactical gear, and she had that same aura of control and action that Holden and the other man from his team had.

"We need to talk." Shay's gaze flicked to Willa. "Alone."

Willa might have wilted at the authoritative look on a different day, but today… "This is my house. If you want alone, you can leave it."

Shay's eyebrows shot up. "It seems you left a few things out of your report, Parker."

Willa had the fascinating view of Holden tensing. She wouldn't say his expression was guilty or defensive, exactly, but it certainly wasn't controlled.

"I have a handle on the situation. I'm not sure why you're here."

Shay eyed Willa again. Willa kept her chin up and her gaze direct. She wasn't going to be afraid or nervous. If Holden wouldn't help her, it was always possible this woman would.

"Did she give you that bump on your head?"

This time Holden's gaze slid to Willa. "Not exactly," he muttered. "Willa. Give us a few."

Willa didn't even bother to respond with words. She crossed her arms over her chest and stayed resolutely where she was. She would not be maneuvered. She would not be…set aside. It felt too much like being a kid again. Set aside so Mom and Dad could handle whatever new job they had to take.

Had to. Couldn't escape their former lives. She'd always believed that. But for a brief, horrible moment, it occurred to her that maybe they just hadn't *wanted* to quit. Not enough.

She shook the thought away. Or tried. Because Shay nodded toward the door and Holden went outside. Shay followed.

Willa was left alone in her house. Out of the loop. Pushed to the side. While a bunch of people she didn't know decided things about her life, and her parents' lives.

She couldn't control them. No, she'd learned that from living with her parents. She couldn't control anyone.

But she could control herself, decide herself and act herself.

So, she would.

HOLDEN STOOD OUT in the pitch-black night feeling unaccountably…caught. Why? He didn't have a clue.

He'd done everything he should have done. Followed protocol.

Maybe he'd left a few details out of the report. Maybe he'd been a little vague when it came to Willa. But that didn't mean he needed Shay to appear on the scene. Nor should he feel anything but competent and ready for the next step now that she was here.

Why was everything so backward? He didn't know, but it had to stop. "I've got it covered. I don't know why you're here."

"You didn't say you'd been hurt," Shay said gravely.

"That's not why you came. You couldn't be here all the way from headquarters this quickly if Gabe dimed me out."

"It's not diming you out to inform your superior of a serious injury. You need a new bandage. There's concussion protocol to follow."

"Hey, Mom? I'm fine."

She didn't laugh. She didn't so much as sigh. "This isn't a joke, Parker. You know the rules."

"Yeah, I know the rules. I also know I'm fine and I know what I'm doing."

"Last mission you stepped in when Sabrina was still fighting because she was injured and you knew it."

"It's a bump. There's also not someone currently attacking me. It's different than what happened with her. You have to know it's different. And we don't have time for this. I've got the bullet. Gabe's got the shells. We need to run tests. We need to move forward before the hit man closes in on the target."

"You don't think she's the target?" Shay said, inclining her head toward the old farmhouse.

Holden looked back at the house. Lights were still on. He knew he'd been fooling himself that Willa would go crawl in bed and sleep, but he'd held out some stupid hope she'd just…let him handle it. "I'm not sure. She's not the only target, if she is one. She thinks it's her parents. They've got connections to spy groups. Including the CIA. Which would have been in my next report, once I'd finished gathering evidence."

"Why do you sound unsure?"

"Something doesn't add up. I can't figure out what. It might be her." Holden thought about the pseudo-bunker belowground. "Can we get Elsie out here?"

"If necessary."

"If there's the potential this connects to the CIA, I don't want anyone but her poking around on the computer Willa's got."

"Willa. That her real name?"

Holden shrugged, trying to sound detached. Because he *was* detached. Even if Willa had saved his life. "Not sure. She might not even be sure. Her parents are spies. After seeing the setup, I believe it. Or maybe I believe they're involved in something. She thinks it's good. But what if it's not? She wouldn't know. She's their daughter."

"Unless she's part of it."

Holden considered. Tried to really, dispassionately

consider it. "It wouldn't fit. I just can't see how her playing me would fit."

"Women have ways to make men think they're weaker than they are."

"I work with you and Sabrina. Who do you take me for?"

Shay seemed to consider that. Then she jerked her chin toward him. "How'd you get the bump?"

He explained the car accident in more detail than he'd given North Star before. Left out the part about Willa chaining him to a bed. It wasn't hiding things. It was just not including information that was neither here nor there. He was out of the chains now.

"This spy thing…"

"She won't give me their names. I'd say you guys could investigate her, but we don't know what our hit man knows. We don't want to bring more suspicion on her. But she's got a fancy computer in that underground bunker of hers. If Elsie can hack into it, she might be able to find things Willa doesn't know or doesn't want to say."

"Will Willa let that happen?"

An idea formed. One he didn't particularly like, but it would get the job done. "If I let her come with me to track down her parents, she won't have to know."

"You can't take a civilian around with you on a dangerous mission."

"She wants to go. She claims her parents taught her some skills." He thought about the way she'd fought him in some attempt to prove she could knock him down first. No, he hadn't fought back, but she'd held her own. "She demonstrated some."

"Gross."

"Get your mind out of the gutter, Shay. I've known this woman less than twenty-four hours."

"Please, Holden. I've seen you work."

Torn between offense and amusement, Holden shook his head. "She tried to fight me. She's okay."

Shay made a considering noise. She studied the house, and Holden knew she'd consider his plan. Pros and cons. Even if she didn't agree, she'd take the time to consider it.

Shay shook her head, and Holden was sure he'd either have to disobey a direct order or find some new, better reasoning for Willa coming with him. Which was more likely: Willa letting them search her computer, or convincing Shay to let him take Willa with him?

He really didn't know.

"You know she's running, right?" Shay said conversationally, rocking back on her heels as she slipped her hands into her pockets.

"Running?"

"I'd lay my life savings that she's already climbing out a window on the other side of the house."

Holden stared at the house. She wouldn't. He didn't exactly expect her to crawl into bed and sleep, but she wouldn't run. She couldn't. "She wouldn't leave her animals."

"You so sure about that?"

He was. He *was*. But he found himself moving

forward anyway. Creeping around the house until the back was in view. He saw no sign of her, but there was an open window, the screen missing. No, not missing. It had been carefully propped up against the house on the ground.

Holden swore. Shay chuckled and slapped him on the back. "She's got your number, Parker. Admit it."

"Like hell," he muttered disgustedly. "Get Elsie here. Get her in that underground computer, whatever it takes. I'll keep Willa busy trying to find her parents. Keep in touch. I want to know anything found the second it's found."

"Anything else?" Shay said blandly, a subtle reminder *she* was the boss, not him. Still, it was his assignment.

"That should do it."

Chapter Ten

Willa moved through the dark with practiced ease. The moonlight helped, but she'd taken this path before.

Maybe Holden didn't believe in her capabilities, but she knew them. She felt a twinge of guilt about leaving her animals behind. She had a plan in place for that too—she was nothing if not prepared—but a neighboring farmer making sure they were fed and watered wasn't the same as being loved.

But it had to be done. Some things just had to be done. Like breaking into her parents' safe and escaping into the night, away from Holden and his *group* and whatever their priorities were.

Her priority was her parents.

She hadn't given them their insisted-upon thirty-six hours, but she thought the existence of a hit man, another secret group, and being shot at meant they'd have to forgive her for engaging in emergency measures early.

It'd take a while to make it to town. The sun would definitely rise before she'd get there. That was okay if she was careful. The RV storage facility where her parents stored their car was pretty isolated. Even in the light of day, it wouldn't be too difficult to sneak in and take it.

She'd have to slow down, though. If she kept running, she'd wear herself out before she completed the long, long trek. But if Holden caught her...

Surely it would take him some time to figure her out. Some time to talk to the woman and make their plans. *Surely* he'd assume she went to bed and leave her to it.

"Don't be an idiot, Willa," she muttered to herself. He'd know. He'd find out. She had only minutes to make her escape count. Luckily, she knew the area and—

She heard the footsteps a second too late. In the next second she was tumbling to the ground, someone tumbling on top of her. She didn't scream. She fought. She would always, *always* fight.

Hands clamped around her wrists, so she used her legs to kick wildly.

"Damn it, Willa. It's me."

She huffed out a breath, as if *that* changed anything. "I know exactly who it is," she said, *almost* landing a knee where he'd definitely be knocked back by the blow. But he shifted at the last second.

They grappled, but all he did was try to grab. There was no attempt to hurt her or even immobilize her. It was like he was dodging blows, waiting for her to get tired or just accept that he'd found her.

"Would you stop?" he gritted out, barely dodging a fist to the nose.

She would have liked to have connected, but he maneuvered her onto her back on the cool, damp ground. He used his legs to clamp her legs together, so she only had her arms to try and escape. No matter how she tried to wiggle away, his legs kept her locked tight.

She could land a very, *very* painful punch in this position, but even as she balled her fist and considered it, he hopped off her.

He flicked on a flashlight, which had her wincing away from the sudden brightness. She lay on the ground and blew out a breath. They'd grappled, and she'd accomplished nothing. But at least he'd accomplished *less* than nothing.

"How do you get by in your job never, ever hurting a woman?"

He didn't say anything to that. He got very quiet and very still, and she remembered what he'd said when she'd said he must not have anyone who loved him. *Direct hit.*

"I can't believe you'd leave your animals," he said, completely ignoring her comment.

She opened her mouth to lecture him about how much *care* she put into her animals, but that would give things away she was trying not to give away. Eventually she got to her feet, brushing off dirt she couldn't see but could feel.

"If you're going to drag me back... Well, you're going to have to fight me. Actually fight me. I won't go back until I've done what I have to do." She balled her fists, got into a fighting stance and readied herself.

He heaved out a sigh. "I'm not going to fight you, Willa."

"Then you have to let me go. I mean, there's no *letting*. I'm going." She started to move, but he only stood in her way. Arms crossed. He held the flashlight, illuminating the area around them enough for her to see his face was smudged with dirt, so hers probably was too.

"You aren't going anywhere. At least, not alone. You don't know where the man who shot at you is. He could be here."

"He could be. And he'd likely fight back."

"He'd shoot you dead."

"You don't know that."

Holden groaned. "You might be the most frustrating woman I've ever met. And maybe if you'd stuck around and actually cooperated—"

"Cooperated? You told me to go to bed! I won't be pushed aside while my parents are in danger. I won't."

"You might have been cordially invited to accompany me," he said dryly.

She opened her mouth to argue, then snapped her mouth shut. Had she been rash? Should she have waited? She narrowed her eyes at him. No. No, that wouldn't have gone the way she wanted, no matter what he claimed.

"You're going to come with me?"

"You're going to come with *me*."

She rolled her eyes. "Do you know where to begin?"

"Do you?"

She thought of the papers in her pocket. Codes again. Codes he wouldn't be able to crack. At least, not quickly. She chewed on her lip, and in the glow of the flashlight his eyes narrowed.

"Willa," he said, a warning tone to his voice. "What do you know?"

She opened her mouth to tell him. It was like second nature, somehow, to want to tell him everything. To be thrilled he was going to work with her on this. She needed to be more careful. More wary of him.

"Let's just consider you on a need-to-know basis. And you don't."

"That doesn't work for me," he said, and his voice had a hard edge to it. But he wouldn't fight her or hurt her. It was hard to be afraid of an edge that wouldn't cut. What must be in his past, she wondered.

"You're not going to threaten it out of me. Or torture it out of me. Why would I tell you anything?"

"So I help you, Willa," he said, sounding irritable.

"Maybe I don't need your help."

"Fine." He turned away from her and started walking back toward her house. He was calling her bluff. That was fine. She didn't need his help. She knew where she was going, and maybe she didn't know what she was doing or how exactly she was going to do it, but she had a target. A place to go. She...

She muttered a swear and then scrambled after him. "Wait. Okay, wait." She didn't *need* his help, but it might come in handy, and didn't her parents deserve as much help as she could offer? He hadn't brought his team along, but he still likely had more resources than she did.

"I'd like your help." When he didn't so much as move a muscle, she sighed. "Please."

"You have to tell me what you know."

"Couldn't you just…let me lead and trust that I know what I'm doing and I'll fill you in as needed?" She knew he wouldn't agree to it, but at least if she'd asked, she didn't feel quite like she'd utterly let down her parents.

"How about we start with the thing you're not telling me."

Willa wanted to pout. How did a man who didn't know her know she was keeping things from him? How had he caught up to her so quickly?

It was just an unfortunate reminder that even if she was capable of weathering threats, she was out of her league when it came to actually ending them.

"I wasn't lying to you before, exactly. I don't know who they work for, and I don't know where they are. But… I do have access to a few answers."

"How? Where?" he demanded.

She didn't need to tell him about the papers. She didn't *need* to tell him anything. She could lie. She *could* lie. Intellectually, she knew she was capable. But emotionally… Well, it just didn't seem possible. "Obviously they knew that their work was dangerous. That something might happen to them and I'd never get appropriate word. So, they always leave me some coded information about who I can contact if I have real cause to believe they're in danger."

She didn't include the other stipulations. She was supposed to wait thirty-six hours. She was supposed to research a few things before she went straight to the source. For their own safety, and hers.

But they'd never, ever given her reason to worry before. There had never been a legitimate reason to take their last resort. She was still struggling with believing she should. Maybe that's why she hadn't actually looked at the information yet. She'd just grabbed it and ran.

Because she'd let emotions win over sense. Over careful thought. She was afraid for her parents, irritated with Holden's high-handedness. Emotions had won, and she'd made mistakes.

She blew out a breath. "How do you do it?"

"Do what?"

"Make decisions without letting your emotions get in the way. Mom and Dad are forever scolding me about it, and I did it again. Felt then acted without thinking it through. I don't know how to turn it off. The feelings. The fear."

"You shouldn't have to do it. You're a civilian."

"I wish. I *wish* it were that simple, but it's not. I'm stuck between two worlds, and I don't fit into either. I don't know how to be comfortable in either. I can't sit around and hope they're okay. I know too much. Understand too much. But I can't shut off how scared I am for them. I can't shut off how much I love them.

So, how can I? How can I lock it all away until it's convenient?"

She stood there waiting for an answer. A magic one that could give her the capability of doing what her parents did.

"I don't know your parents, Willa, but they left you with some elaborate underground compound. That doesn't strike me as something people who can shut off their emotions do. If they really shut emotion off, wouldn't they have given you up for adoption or something to keep you far away from them?"

Willa didn't know what to say to that. It kind of made her want to cry. She knew her parents loved her, but they left her so often. They'd put her in danger before and likely would again. Sometimes she wondered if they just...loved their life a little more than her.

But Holden, a man she barely knew, had a point. That point brought up *more* emotion. Tenderness toward her parents, and maybe even a little toward Holden.

Holden, who was going to help her. Or maybe he was going to use her, but if it got her to her parents, did it matter? "There's a car. At a storage facility for RVs and boats. Outside town. It's a trek, but I figure whoever was shooting at me wouldn't be able to track me to that vehicle. Not right away, anyway."

"And then what?"

"Then I'd follow their code. I'm not sure what it'll lead me to. Them? Their superiors? Something else entirely? I don't have a clue. I can only follow it and hope I'm wrong—and not so right I lead the bad guys right to their doorstep."

He inclined his head. "Solid plan. Lead the way."

She blinked. Once. He…was agreeing to her plan? *And* letting her lead? She opened her mouth to ask if he was sure, but then closed it. She didn't need him to be sure. *She was sure.*

So, she began to walk. She knew where she was going, though she considered taking a circular route in case this was some kind of trap. It felt like one. He'd agreed too easily. Especially after arguing with her about partnering up not that long ago.

"The woman…"

"Shay?"

"Yes, her. She's…okay with you working with me?"

"*Okay* isn't the word I'd use. She agreed. Reluctantly."

"Why?"

"You have information I don't."

He said it so matter-of-factly she had no choice but to believe him. He saw her less as a partner or leader and more as the means with which to get the information he needed. Which didn't bother her. She hadn't yet proved to him just how good of a partner she could be.

But she would.

They walked. Walked and walked. Sometimes she tried to engage Holden in conversation, but he almost always turned it into asking her more about her parents and what she knew about what they did.

They continued to walk, even as the dark of night began to slowly lighten into the glow of dawn. Willa took a deep breath of almost-morning air. She was often awake at this time, tending to her animals. She loved the otherworldliness of it. The stillness. The light that no other part of day could quite emulate.

"Must you hum?" Holden muttered grumpily.

"It's just such a beautiful morning."

"It'd be a hell of a lot more beautiful in bed. Asleep."

"Once we get to the car, you can take a nice little nap." She took in her surroundings, satisfied with the progress they were making. "We're getting close. I'll want you to stay out of sight while I get the car. I think I can sneak it out without anyone seeing me, but if I do get caught, it'll be a lot easier to talk my way out of it with Earl if I'm alone."

He eyed her disapprovingly. "You've proven you're a flight risk."

"Don't be silly."

"You've run away from me once. You won't run away from me again."

An odd shiver ran through her at the seriousness in his tone. Odd because it wasn't fear or worry. It wasn't even foreboding. It felt a bit like anticipation, and that didn't make *any* sense.

So she ignored it. "You'll be able to see me the whole time. Besides, if I run, I have no doubt you'll find a way to follow me and pretend like you're the big, bad wolf who's going to really punish me this time, while dodging punches and telling me to *quit it*."

Cheerful despite the lack of sleep, she went back to humming but only got about a half a step farther before Holden grabbed her by the arm. It was unexpected, and not gentle, but not a rough grab, either. He seemed to excel at touches that were powerful without being threatening.

"I want you to be very clear about one thing, Willa," he said, his voice cold and authoritative. "I don't hurt women. I won't. But I'd incapacitate you if it became necessary."

Despite the chill in his voice, his hand was big and warm and gentle. She smiled. She couldn't help it. "Of course you would," she said indulgently. She even patted his hand. He likely had to believe it. A man like him had to believe he was the strongest person in the room. And he was. No doubt he was stronger than her, but if he refused to do little more than roll around and hold on to a woman's arms or legs, he'd never actually *incapacitate* her or any other woman.

The world tilted, and suddenly she was on her back, but…gently. Nothing jarred. It wasn't like falling. Because no matter that Holden had knocked her off her feet, he'd also somehow cushioned the blow.

Which didn't really prove his point. She supposed the way one of his large hands cuffed hers together over her head was supposed to prove it for him, but that just meant he was leaning over her. Looking at her with an odd light of triumph in those dark blue eyes of his.

She didn't feel incapacitated. She felt…alive. Like

every nerve ending sparked with energy. That triumph in his gaze faded into something else.

And his gaze dropped to her mouth.

HOLDEN WONDERED IF a head injury could cause a person to detach from their own body. To have a personality transplant. To be changed utterly and completely just because a woman he could damn well take down, but wouldn't, acted like he was *cute* for explaining the truth to her.

He was a man who enjoyed women, when time allowed, but a certain kind of woman. Not a guileless farm girl who somehow had secrets and spies in her family and looked up at him when he'd knocked and held her down as if he was holding her hand.

How could he be attracted to freckles, and a nose just a shade too close to sharp? Her hair was like gold in the pale light of dawn, and her eyes that deep, mesmerizing green. Her mouth…

Holden jumped to his feet so fast he nearly tripped over himself. But there was no way he could…

No way. It was just a trick of the pearly dawn and…his head injury. It had to be that.

Not just…her.

She leveraged up on her elbows, still lying sprawled on the ground where he'd taken her down. To prove a point.

Why could he never seem to prove a point with this woman? He was an accomplished field agent and had been for years. After all the mistakes of his early adulthood, he hadn't made any for years. He'd honed himself into a machine. Machines didn't make mistakes because women were…

Whatever she was.

"Why are you looking at me like I'm a snake?"

Snakes were a hell of a lot less dangerous than this woman. "How far are we from the car?"

She got to her feet, and though he had half a thought to help her up, he kept his hands deep in his pockets.

"You know, I'm not a total shut-in," she said, brushing the dirt from her pants.

"Huh?"

"I went to school. Off and on. I even had a boyfriend my junior year of high school. Terrible kisser, but, you know, he did actually kiss me." She pulled a face. "He was not *good* at it."

"Why are you—"

"And that was like seven years ago—my junior year, that is—so I'm not as young as I look."

"I didn't—"

"So, don't start treating me like I'm some kind of freak. Life's been weird, but I'm not some wolf child who doesn't know anything about life outside my menagerie of animals. I *like* animals, but that doesn't mean I'm completely…" She trailed off, clearly frustrated with her lack of having a word for whatever she wanted to say.

"I don't know what you're talking about," he replied.

And he didn't. More or less. Maybe he hadn't pegged her at twenty-four, but not too far off. And he'd never considered that she'd been totally sheltered. She seemed to know how to deal with him just fine.

"I know what I seem like. But I'm not…that. I'm not naive. I'm not incompetent. And most important, I'm not stupid. You'll need to understand that and believe it." She set her gaze to the east. "I'd say we have a mile left. Let's not waste daylight."

She started marching and Holden followed, not sure what else to do in the situation. If he tried to explain himself, it'd be overkill. And show too much of what he'd been thinking back there when his only thoughts could be the assignment at hand.

But the words were there. The explanations. The excuses. And the strangest urge to lay them all at her feet, when he was much more comfortable keeping complicated emotions to himself.

They walked the last mile in silence. As the storage place came into view—nothing more than a big field with a tall chain-link fence around it and a tiny office situated in front of the gate of the fence—Willa's pace got slower. Until she came to a complete stop.

"You'll need to stay out of sight. You see the road there? Keep walking down it. Pretend you're a hitchhiker." She gave him a once-over, her mouth curving. "You kind of look like one."

He gave her a doleful look that had her chuckling. He schooled away the smile he wanted to give in response. "I'm not letting you out of my sight, Willa."

"Just to get the car. You walk down that way, and I'll get the car and drive and pick you up. I can't guarantee no one's in the office, even if it is early, and I don't think it's wise to let anyone see you. Especially if someone out there is looking for me. I get the car, I meet you down the road a little ways. Stick your thumb out. Voilà."

Holden studied her. He didn't think she was lying. That was her plan, and she was right. It was best for their purposes, if someone was following her, if they thought she was alone. Vulnerable.

She wouldn't be. He'd be damned if he'd let her be. But that didn't mean he felt comfortable walking away from her while she went to get a vehicle. It would be far too easy for her to take off, and then he'd lose more precious time trying to track her down.

Time that could lead to her parents or whoever else was the target ending up dead, and no matter that it'd be her fault, he'd feel like he had blood on his hands.

Hands she took in hers. A surprisingly firm gesture. Maybe a little desperate. "You're going to have to trust me," she said, squeezing his fists with her much smaller hands. "We're going to have to trust each other. We can't work knowing the other person is keeping secrets."

It should be of no consequence to him that she was a liar. That no matter how entreating her gaze was, or how oddly comforting her hand on his was, she lied. And it hurt. Which made the words that came out of his mouth next far too bitter for the situation. "But you are keeping secrets, Willa."

Chapter Eleven

"Holden." She didn't know what else to say. Yes, she had a few secrets. She'd phrased that poorly. She'd only wanted his trust. His partnership.

Maybe she was letting her loneliness get in the way of good sense. More feelings when she was supposed to school them all away.

She dropped his hands, feeling vaguely slimy. Like she was the one in the wrong. "Then I'll trust you first," she said, squinting her eyes against the rising sun. She couldn't predict what he'd do. She could only control herself.

Herself. Someone who couldn't escape her emotions. No, she couldn't. Maybe it was time to stop fighting them. Maybe she had to *trust* them. "I trust you, Holden. I'm going to trust you to realize the best option is for you to start walking down the street and for me to meet you a ways down and pick you up. If you don't, well… Then I was wrong about you and I'll have to live with it."

She started walking away from him. She was desperate to look back, to see what he would do, but it would only undermine her point.

No matter who she wanted to be, or what world she felt more comfortable in, deep down she wasn't the image she gave off.

If he'd wanted to kiss her, and part of her desperately wanted to believe that's what that moment had been, he wanted to kiss the damsel in distress. The weak, innocent, too-young-looking woman who loved animals more than people and wanted a simple life free of the fear and danger of her parents' lives.

She *wished* she could be that simple. She *wished* that's who she was.

But it wasn't.

She approached the gate to the storage area. She peered in the little office building, but the lights were off and the hours clearly stated. She glanced at the little security camera pointed at the gate. Likely there were more on the inside.

That didn't bother her so much. She knew the owners, and while she knew they wouldn't appreciate her breaking in, she was taking what belonged to her parents. She could probably sweet-talk them out of pressing charges.

Maybe.

She bit her lip. Charges didn't actually worry her in the overall sense. But if law enforcement put some kind of flag on the car, she'd have the kind of police interest she didn't need when she was trying to sneak somewhere to help her parents.

"Taken care of."

Willa whirled around at Holden's voice. He was shoving his phone into his pocket and going straight for the lock on the gate. "Security cameras are down. It'll be explained to the owners as maintenance from the security system. We'll get a replacement car in here within the hour to make it look like your parents' car wasn't taken."

He picked the lock in under ten seconds and was shoving open the gate.

"How—"

"Oh, and there are two operatives who are going to stay at your farm and take care of your animals, so you don't have to worry about whoever you were going to call to help on that score."

He was walking into the storage area, and she was rooted to the same spot. "How did you…"

"Come on now. No time to dawdle. We have to be out of here in five minutes or the cameras will come back on."

She looked up at the security camera. She supposed there'd be plenty of time to ask him how he'd done any of it.

She had to remember she was dealing with a man like her parents. He had contacts and access to all sorts of things she'd never understand. She might be able to hold her own, but he could flip the game. She wouldn't be able to beat him, but she could keep up. If she kept herself ready to take whatever change, whatever surprise came her way.

So, she led him to her parents' car. Before she could open the driver's side door, he did. She scowled at him. "I'm driving. You don't know where you're going."

"Do you?" he countered, holding his hand out, presumably for the keys.

She wanted to drive. She wanted to stay in control. She wanted to run this and have him follow her around and step in only when necessary.

Of course it wouldn't happen like that. She was the tagalong, help-only-when-necessary part of this partnership. It grated, but for now, she'd just have to swallow her pride a little bit.

It was for her parents. She would do anything to make sure they were safe. Even hand him the keys and then walk around to slide into the passenger seat.

He started the engine immediately and was driving through the rows of RVs and boats to the gate.

She didn't need to be told to get out and lock it back up behind them when he paused outside the facility. Ideally, no one would ever know they'd been here.

Ideally.

"Are you sure you can get a replacement in? We want to be as under the radar as we can possibly be. If the car is flagged as stolen…"

"I'm sure," Holden said simply. "Now, which way?"

"Head east for right now. Just stay on this road."

"We're going to need to stop and get some gas."

"There's a station about ten miles along this road. Just get going."

He did so, and Willa had to decide if she'd pull

out the papers here in the car, or in the bathroom at the gas station.

She'd asked him to trust her. She'd said they had to trust each other. Even while she'd been keeping secrets. Secrets he'd seen through.

She studied his profile as he drove. He was classically handsome. All square jaw and high cheekbones. The stubble that had grown in overnight gave him a rough edge, even with the slight cleft in his chin, but his eyes were so blue he somehow still looked... very close to regal. She could picture him in a suit, or something equally elegant. As easily as she could picture him in jeans and a T-shirt enjoying a drink in a bar.

He was a man who could slide into surroundings and have pretty much anyone eating out of the palm of his hand.

Including you.

She didn't like that feeling, even being sure just about anyone would fall for it. But she was hardly *anyone*. She was the daughter of spies.

Spies who needed her help.

She was torn between what they'd want her to do and what *she* wanted to do. But hadn't she learned a long time ago she wasn't them? Couldn't be them. So, she had to be herself. Trust herself. And against her will, she trusted Holden Parker of some secretive group.

She'd saved his life. He'd attempted to save hers. They had to do this hand in hand, and she couldn't expect his hand if she didn't put hers in his.

Nicole Helm   127

She dug the papers out of her pocket and spread them over her lap.

"It's in code."

She hadn't even noticed him glance her way, but she was used to that kind of unnoticed split focus. "Of course it's in code."

"Do you know how to break it?"

Now she spared him a killing glance. She could stand him underestimating her, but honestly.

"Okay, okay, you can break it," he muttered, eyes back on the road. "How long?"

"Ten, fifteen minutes. Just keep driving. Stop at the gas station when we get to it. We'll go from there."

HOLDEN DROVE, ONE eye on the road, the other on Willa. She focused on the paper in front of her, and whatever decoding she did was in her head. She was wilting, though, exhaustion beginning to stamp itself across her face.

She'd need a nap once she could tell him where they were going. He opened his mouth to ask her how close she was, then closed it. He had a feeling she'd get that flinty, offended look again, and he…

Well, he wasn't sure why that affected him, but it did. He didn't like it. Irritated he was changing the way he did things, demanded things, because of her *feelings*, he focused fully on the road in front of him. Everything around them was flat, and he could see the gas station sign in the distance.

Summer sunlight shimmered across the concrete and the fields on either side. It was pretty country, he had to admit. Prettier still if you were looking for a kind of peace. *He* wasn't, of course, but he understood why Willa would be searching for some.

"Why Nebraska?" he found himself asking, when he should be quiet and let her work.

She lifted her head from the paper, squinted into the sunny morning. "Well, my choices were limited to an extent. It had to be somewhere small, out of the way. A place people wouldn't happen upon."

"I'm not saying Nebraska doesn't make sense for that, but so do a lot of states."

She slid a glance his way, as if considering to tell him something important. "I know you said your parents are…passed, but you knew them. You knew who you were and where you came from?"

He wanted to evade that question, but it wasn't fair when he'd asked a personal one of his own. "My parents weren't close to theirs."

"But you know who they were. You knew if your ancestors were immigrants or Revolutionary War heroes or what have you."

Holden didn't. Not because he hadn't been able to, just because it hadn't been a topic they'd discussed. Holden's parents had moved away from their own parents, and the contact had been limited and tense. He'd never wondered about *history*. He'd only been concerned with his mother living.

Then she hadn't.

"I wasn't allowed to know," Willa was saying. "I'm not supposed to know. The names my parents use aren't the names they were given by theirs."

Holden's eyebrows raised. "That sounds like you know."

"I figured it out. When I still thought I might follow in their footsteps and be a spy. I was about twelve, and we'd settled in a place in Indiana where I went to middle school for seventh and eighth grade. My classmates were doing projects about their grandparents. I had nothing. So I set out to find something."

"Without your parents knowing?"

Willa nodded. "Sometimes I have to wonder, because of what they do and who they are, if they let me find out what I wanted to know. If it was…a cookie crumb of sorts. Regardless, I found it. I traced my ancestors as best I could. Civil War heroes and revolutionaries. You name it, they did it, and then for some reason, in the 1870s, they moved from Maine to Nebraska. Became farmers and lived quiet lives. My grandfather didn't even fight in World War II. I could never find out why they moved, why they changed. Maybe even if my father hadn't cut ties with his family for whatever reasons he did, I'd know. Or maybe I wouldn't. But I found a place not too far from where they settled and started to farm."

Holden tried to absorb all that and file it away as information about her, and her parents. No feeling. Just facts.

But it painted such a…picture. A young woman who wanted roots.

He'd lost all contact with his sisters and brothers. First because of the state, and then because he'd been labeled *bad* because of his connections to the

Sons. He'd lost due to fate, and then he'd lost due to his own dumb decisions.

He thought about Sabrina, and a few other people he'd stumbled upon and brought into the North Star fold. Because they'd reminded him of himself.

Because they'd felt like a way to make up for his past mistakes.

Willa wasn't trying to do that, but it had a similar impetus behind it. Reaching out for connection. For some tie...since they couldn't have ties of their own.

Willa rubbed her eyes. "This code is particularly difficult. I guess it makes sense. It'd have to be a real emergency for me to want to pound my head against this." She yawned and looked out at the upcoming gas station. "Coffee. I definitely need some coffee. But we'll keep heading east until I can figure this out."

"You're tired."

"I'll muddle through." She shrugged as they pulled into the gas station. "Gotta figure this out before we rest."

He stopped in front of a gas pump. She studied him and frowned. "You need a hat to cover up that bandage. People will remember that. Some people might even ask questions. You want to blend in."

She was right about that. He had a lot of things in his pack, but he didn't think he had a hat.

She reached into the back seat and picked up a hat with a mesh back that read *Haines Feed Store*.

She plopped it on his head, gently pulling it down and over the bandage. She studied him with serious green eyes. "There." Her mouth curved. "You almost fit in."

"Almost?"

"I'm not sure you could ever look like a farmer, Holden. But the hat helps you look less...lethal." She patted his shoulder and moved to get out of the car, but she was holding on to that piece of paper with the code.

He narrowed his eyes, grabbing her arm before she could slide out. When she looked back at him, frowning, he refused to let himself feel guilty about being suspicious.

"You can't run," he said sternly.

She met his gaze, all open innocence. "I'm not going to run." She dropped the piece of paper in the console between them as if it hadn't been her plan to take it with her in the first place. Then she got out of the car and walked into the convenience store.

He believed her, though he probably shouldn't.

But that didn't mean he trusted her yet.

Chapter Twelve

Willa couldn't stop yawning. There was a sign on the door about not using the bathroom without buying something, so she stared at the cooler full of caffeinated drinks. She wanted coffee, but the gas station fare left a lot to be desired, so she'd have to settle for a soft drink.

If she could engage her mind enough to pick one.

She had to stay awake long enough to crack the code. She was usually really adept at it, but this one was tough. Or she was that tired.

Or she was that afraid, knowing her parents had purposefully made it a challenge because they didn't want her coming after them half-cocked. Maybe they'd made it impossible. Maybe it was a lie.

She wanted to lean her forehead against the cool glass and have a good cry. And then sleep for twelve hours straight. At least. Then she wanted to wake up and have this all be a dream.

The door she'd been all but leaning against opened, and she had to step back. Holden pulled out a variety of soft drink bottles. "There. That should do it. Come on. You're dead on your feet."

She wanted to argue with him, but of course he was right. "How come you aren't?"

"Practice," he returned simply.

She wanted to grumble and pout, but they got up to the checkout counter and she forced a polite smile at the cashier.

"I need to use the bathroom."

The woman eyed her then pulled out a big pipe from underneath the counter. A tiny key dangled off it. "Round back," she said with a smoker's rasp as she began to ring up Holden's purchases.

Willa took the ridiculous "key fob" and walked out of the gas station. It was mostly empty. There was an old man in overalls—no shirt—walking his dog down the scraggly sidewalk in front of the gas station, but that was it. No cars drove by.

Willa let out a breath and tried to roll away some of the tension in her shoulders. No one was following them. She just had to figure out the code and they could get to her parents. If they didn't stop anymore, surely she could get to them before they were hurt.

This wasn't about killing. Whoever had shot at them hadn't killed her, and if they *wanted* her it was to threaten her parents. To get something out of them.

She rounded the corner of the station to the back. There were two cars parked here. She'd only seen one worker in the gas station, but that didn't mean someone hadn't been in the back. Both cars were unremarkable, aging sedans that fit the means of the workers.

Willa studied the two doors on the back side of the building—rusting and sun worn—the signs between men and women so faded she could barely make them out. Still, she'd spent enough time on the road to know that she wanted the women's bathroom—they were cleaner. Always.

Of course, *cleaner* didn't mean clean. Willa wrinkled her nose as she stepped inside the dark, dank bathroom. There was one lone lightbulb to flick on— no windows to let in the sunlight.

The floor was sticky, the sink rusted, the soap dispenser empty. On a sigh, she did what she had to do and then attempted to wash her hands the best she could. She hoped she could get a shower soon. Maybe scrub herself with bleach.

On another yawn, she grabbed the pipe and opened the door back into the bright day. She squinted against the sun before stepping forward.

The blast of pain was so sudden, so fierce she stumbled back. Which gave her a second to gather her wits before the man stepped in the doorway of the bathroom. She hadn't dropped the pipe, so she used it.

She didn't know what he'd done to her head. Punched her or hit her with something, but she knew if he got her in here and closed the door, she would be in some serious trouble. She was having trouble seeing with it being so bright outside and so dark in the small bathroom, so she could only swing the pipe wildly and try to use it as the worst weapon she could muster as she pressed forward.

She would not be pushed back into this bathroom. She would not go down that easily. She could fight. She wouldn't panic. The circumstances weren't comfortable, but self-protecting wasn't supposed to be. If she could just get him out into the sunlight, her eyes could adjust and she'd stop feeling like she was fighting blind.

She pushed. She whacked the pipe against the man. He grunted but got one meaty, sweaty hand wrapped around her arm and jerked her backward. She slid a bit, but immediately charged. No, no, she would not be stuck in this gross room to die.

She pushed. She hit. At one point, she bit. That had the man howling out in shocked pain, and it gave her the chance to push past him and out into the bright light of day. She knew he'd followed, was on her heels. But she was at least free from the horrible-smelling room.

Now she could *really* fight.

Finally.

"Now you're going to regret it." Something hot and sticky dripped into her eye, but she blinked it away and held her fists up. She realized then he had a gun strapped to his hip. But he wasn't using it.

He wanted her alive. It was both relief and irritation. Oh, he was sure as hell not getting her alive.

She advanced. Her first kick wasn't meant to hurt, but to knock the gun off the holster on his side. It didn't work, but it had him thinking about the gun.

He grappled for it, and as he did she slammed a fist into his face as hard as she could.

The gun toppled to the ground as he brought his hands up to his face. Clearly, he didn't think she could fight. He hadn't anticipated *this*. They never did.

So, she didn't let up. She punched, she kicked, she shoved, until he was back in the bathroom and she was outside. She slammed the door shut as he tried to reach out and stop her. The scream of pain echoed across the quiet morning, though it was muffled almost immediately as she managed this time to get the door completely shut. She shoved the pipe into the handle of the door so that he wouldn't be able to push out. "You messed with the wrong spy's daughter," she muttered, leaning against the door as she tried to catch her breath and fight off the dizziness stealing over her.

She flipped around and leaned her back against the door. She needed to get away from here, but her energy seemed to drain from her body all at once.

Holden skidded around the corner, gun drawn and murder in his gaze. She might have been afraid if her head didn't hurt so much. "About time," she muttered.

Something flickered in his gaze, but then it was gone. "You're bleeding," he said flatly.

"Yeah, you should see the other guy." She wasn't sure how much longer she'd last on her own two feet, so she didn't reach up and touch the spot on her head that hurt like hell. That would likely send her into a full-fledged faint, and she wasn't going to do that in front of Holden.

"He's in the bathroom," she managed, breathing through the weird haze around her vision.

"Move aside," he said in that same cold, flat tone of voice.

She moved out of his way, didn't even think about questioning him. She was too busy trying to remain upright.

THERE WAS RAGE. There was guilt. So many familiar feelings piling up in his chest, but at the center was something worse.

Fear.

There was a trickle of blood down Willa's face, and she was pale. If he had to guess, she was barely managing not to pass out.

She'd fought off someone and locked him in a bathroom, and Holden didn't want to tear whoever it was limb from damn limb until there was nothing left. Not in the moment.

He wanted to scoop her up and get her away from here. He wanted to deposit her back at her farm and keep her safe and sound. He wanted to erase the wounds on her face and comfort her. *Heal* her. Apologize, prostrate, for ever having let her out of his sight.

He wanted, so desperately, to make it okay.

But that wasn't his job.

He jerked the pipe out of the door handle and opened the door, leading with his gun barrel.

The man sat on his butt in the middle of the bathroom. His face was bleeding, his hand hung at an odd angle. He looked up at Holden with venom in his gaze. "I don't care if I die."

It was a bluff. Holden could read the terror in the man's gaze. Maybe surprise that Willa wasn't such an easy target. He was trying to put on a brave face, but he was *terrified* of dying.

Which meant he didn't think he'd die by failing this mission. Odd. Still, Holden would play the game. "Then it's good I'm not going to kill you," Holden replied, though he held the gun pointed at the man. Not at his chest or head as the man might have expected. "Just shoot off an important piece of anatomy."

The man covered his hands over his crotch, eyes widening. "Hey."

"Three seconds to tell me what you know." All the ocean of feelings inside him had been cordoned off. His voice was mostly flat. If there was any inflection, it was pure violence.

"The cops'll come. That cashier knows you're the only one who's—"

"Three."

"—been here. You'll be wanted for murder."

"Two."

"You don't know what you're getting yourself into here, son. Just let me go and—"

"One," Holden said with a shrug, flicking the safety off the gun.

"All right! Don't…" The man huddled in the corner of the stinky, scummy bathroom and held up his hands. "You can have her. I know they put an open call out and all, but a couple grand isn't enough to kill another guy over. Come on, man. We're all just trying to make a buck."

Holden's brain scrambled to put that information together. Open call. So, he wasn't the only one after Willa. He glanced at her quickly. She still stood right there, looking like death.

Your fault, Parker.

He looked back at the man. Open call. A couple grand. "Funny, I met another guy who said the same thing. He made the mistake of getting in my way."

"I won't. Promise. I've got other jobs. You take the girl." He held up his clearly broken hand. "Too much trouble. I don't want her. I'd take a percentage…" The main trailed off as Holden's finger curled around the trigger.

"Okay, okay. No percentage. You take her and drop her off. You take the money. Just let me go and I'll disappear."

Drop-off. "Where'd they tell *you* to drop her off? Because the last guy either had a different point, or he was lying to me." Holden shrugged. "I don't like it when people lie to me."

"Different…" The man didn't even try to hide his confusion. "You mean they're giving us different ones?"

Holden shrugged. "Seems like. Which one they give you?"

His expression went cagey. "Which one they give you?"

"Who's got the gun, smart guy? I…incapacitated

the last guy who didn't answer me. I'll do the same to you. No skin off my nose."

"For a couple grand? Surely you aren't that desperate," the man said, a wheedling note to his voice.

"Think again, friend."

"Fine. Whatever. I'm out of this one. Killdare Wildlife Refuge. Lake three."

Holden nodded. "Guess the last guy was lying to me. You'll live." But Holden slammed the door and shoved the pipe back in the handle. It immediately began to rattle.

"Hey! Hey, let me out of here." The man banged on the door, but Holden slid his arm around Willa's waist and pulled her forward. "We got to get out of here and quick. Can you jog or do you want me to carry you?"

"I can…"

But Holden didn't bother. She wasn't steady on her feet, so he swept her up into his arms.

"Hey," she protested—weakly at best.

He carried her to the car, hoping they could get out of here before the cashier wondered where her bathroom key had gone. He carried Willa all the way to the car and deposited her in the passenger seat.

He resisted every urge to check her wounds, to buckle her up. They had to get out of here before the police got involved.

He skirted the hood and got in the driver's side. The cashier was coming out the front door of the station, yelling at them to stop.

Holden didn't stop. He got in the car and drove. Fast.

He had to get away from here, and any police inter-ference. Then he'd figure out where to go from there.

"Hey. Eyes open," he said sharply when hers started to droop. "Where's this nature area?"

"I don't know," she mumbled.

"Yes, you do. You need to tell me how to get there."

She blinked, straightening in her seat. "I'm not fa-miliar with it. It can't be around here."

Holden swore under his breath. "Grab my phone and search for it, Willa."

She slumped again. "My head hurts."

"I know. I know it does." He bit back an endear-ment and had to fight the desperate need to stop the car and take care of her wounds. But they had to get somewhere safe. "But you don't want to pass out, do you?"

"No." She blinked a few times, squinted. She lifted her hand.

"Don't do that," he said sharply, and she dropped her hand before touching the gash on her forehead. "Grab the phone. Look up Killdare Wildlife Refuge."

She blew out a breath and grabbed his phone. He watched her out of the corner of one eye, keeping his attention on the road as much as he could.

Her fingers were clumsy, but she tapped some-thing into his phone. She squinted at the screen. "It's up in the corner."

"What corner?" Holden demanded. Every ounce of energy was centered on making himself keep going.

"You know. The corner." She made a vague hand motion. "South Dakota. Wyoming. That corner."

Holden frowned. Nebraska meeting South Dakota and Wyoming. There weren't any decent-size towns in that area, but he wasn't familiar with the wildlife refuge either. Worse, that was hours away.

But he did know of a North Star safe house in that general area. They could get there, duck out of police notice and patch her up. Regroup. Come up with a plan.

He glanced at her, still squinting at his phone. She was bloody and there were bruises already blooming on her face and neck. It made him want to tear something apart. Or maybe turn back around and go ahead and shoot the moron in the bathroom.

But they couldn't do that. Especially if the cashier had already called the police.

"You'll tell me if you feel sick," Holden ordered, increasing his speed as he put his full focus on the road in front of him. "If your vision doubles. Anything majorly off, you tell me. And for the love of God, don't try to touch it."

"You're so bossy," she said grumpily. "Do you think my parents are there? At this refuge?"

"No. He was supposed to drop you off. Doubtful they're there."

"He wasn't anybody, was he? Just some random… bad guy. Trying to get paid. He didn't know anything. He's not the real threat."

"He did enough of a number on you."

She shook her head, then winced. "I was paying attention. I looked at the cars. The people. He shouldn't have been there."

"But he was. That ambush could have killed you."

She made a scoffing sound. "I don't see how. I kicked his butt with no help from you."

Holden wasn't sure how he'd ever live with those minutes of buying drinks and snacks and taking his sweet time to check on her. When he knew they were in danger... He'd just been so sure they were too sneaky...

They *had* been. No one could have followed them. Something was off. So off.

Unless someone knew she'd go for that car in the storage facility. He slid her a look. She was deathly pale and bleeding. He could hardly float the idea her parents were giving the wrong people information about her when she was beaten up.

Because of him.

Worse than even that, there was the fact ammunition had been delivered to Evening, and that moron in the bathroom hadn't used it. Hadn't had it on him.

Was there someone else? Someone not so bad at their job. Someone who knew something. Someone who was tracking them, even now?

Holden checked his rearview mirror. No signs of a tail, but that didn't mean they were in the clear.

"You see a town up there called Vollmer? That's where we're headed. You navigate. Back roads as much as possible."

"I just want to go to sleep," she said, sounding so sad he thought his heart might crack in two.

But he didn't have time to have a heart right now. "You'll stay awake, Willa. One way or another. Now. Where should I turn next?"

Chapter Thirteen

Willa's head was pounding. She felt sweaty and nauseous. Still, she stared at the map on Holden's phone and told him where to go. She didn't mention wanting to puke. Or how badly she wanted a drink of water or a bottle of pain relievers.

She just told him where to go. She understood how important it was for them to get out of range of the police. There was no doubt in her mind the cashier had called the police. No doubt in her mind she would have given a very good description of Holden and Willa to the police at that.

They'd been driving for hours, though. It felt like days. Still, no one had stopped them. And they hadn't stopped. Holden drove a bit like a bat out of hell, and every bump jarred her quickly stiffening body.

But she could tell they'd made some progress. There were trees now. Far more rock outcroppings than there were back in Evening.

"Hand me the phone," he ordered.

He'd been so stiff and authoritative the whole drive. She understood it was because there was a danger they didn't understand and couldn't predict. Because he had a lead, and now he needed to follow it.

And she suspected he was being so…uptight because she'd been hurt. She didn't know why that'd make him all robotic, but she couldn't ignore the fact he hadn't acted like this the whole time—even after she'd tried to beat him with a fire poker.

Still, she was too…drained and hurting and miserable to try and fight with him right now. She handed him the phone and didn't even complain when he kept driving like crazy with one eye on his phone.

He took a couple unexpected turns that had her entire body jostling as he went off-road.

"What on earth are you…" She trailed off as a small cabin, completely surrounded by trees, came into view. He didn't slow up, and the car stopped just inches away from the front door.

"Where are we?"

He didn't answer, just got out of the car. She moved to follow, pushing open the door, but he was there before she'd gotten it half-open. He had her up in his arms again before she could move.

She could walk and she opened her mouth to tell him so, but she wanted desperately to simply lay her head against his shoulder and go to sleep, knowing she'd be safe here—in his arms. The image was so appealing, and everything hurt, so she just…let herself. Rest her head on him, close her eyes and let him take her wherever. She didn't even open her eyes when he stepped into the cabin. She let herself drift until he was putting her down on a surprisingly soft mattress.

"Don't go to sleep," he said sharply. But her eyes were drifting closed again, and sleep seemed like a wonderful alternative to…everything.

She vaguely heard him banging around in another room. It kept her from fully falling to sleep, but she could still kind of float in a weird, gray, exhausted, pained space.

Until he took her by the shoulders. She'd lain down and didn't quite remember it, but he pulled her into a sitting position. When she opened her eyes, he was scowling at her. But his face was close and his eyes were on hers.

So incredibly blue. She'd seen multiple oceans, seen the bright blue of a tropical island. She'd seen so many blues the world had to offer, and still his eyes reminded her of a Nebraska winter sky, on the days the wind was so cold it felt like knives, but also like the world was hers and hers alone.

Then he pushed something against the throbbing pain on her temple, and she yelped in surprise. Then groaned at the stinging burn of what she could only assume was some kind of antiseptic.

He did it again, and she tried to bat his hands away. "Stop that," she said to him, trying to squirm out of his reach.

"You stop that," he returned, holding her in place with one arm. "I've got to clean you up."

"Use water," she said, still trying to fight him

off, though she didn't have much energy to put any strength behind it.

"Sit still," he ordered through gritted teeth. "You had a fight in a middle-of-nowhere gas station bathroom. You're lucky I'm not dropping you into a tub of bleach."

Willa grimaced, suddenly feeling ten times grimier than she had. "I need a shower."

"You need to sit still and let me make sure there aren't any serious injuries here." When she tried to wiggle away from him again, he blew out a breath. "Was I such a baby when you were bandaging me up?"

"You were unconscious."

"I can arrange it."

"Big talk," she muttered. Then sighed. "I guess we're going to have matching head wounds."

He grunted, still prodding at the pain in her head. It still stung, but not with the same force. He lifted her hair out of the way, this way and that. "I think you should be okay without stitches," he muttered before dropping her hair. He studied her face with narrowed eyes, and then his hand was on her cheek. "Does anything else hurt?" he demanded, holding her face gently and staring at her fiercely, practically nose to nose.

Her whole body hurt, and she wondered just what he'd do if she told him that. Would he touch her everywhere?

Honestly, Willa, is now the time for silly fantasies?

She didn't mind making time for them usually, even when in danger, but her heart was thudding dangerously against her chest, and she couldn't break the moment. If he didn't, she was liable to do something incredibly stupid. Like touch him back. "It was a fight, Holden. I won."

He muttered something truly filthy and then, in direct contrast to his swearing, gently laid his forehead against hers, his big, rough hand still cupping her cheek.

She was almost afraid to move, afraid to breathe. He was touching her with such gentle reverence, like she meant something to him, and she wanted…

Well, she wanted that. Even more when his mouth touched hers. It was light. Featherlight. The gentlest touch of lips.

Her eyes fluttered closed, and she sank into it. Hey, he started it. Why not apply a little pressure, fit her bottom lip at the seam of his lips. Reach out, slowly and gently so as not to break the moment, and rest her hands on his shoulders.

He was so tense there, and yet his mouth was still gentle on hers.

"I'm…sorry." The words were unexpected, but any sting she might have felt by them was completely undercut by the fact his lips were still touching hers… as if he couldn't quite bring himself to pull away.

"For what?" she asked, a little too breathlessly, making sure her lips didn't leave his until he did the pulling away.

He pushed off the bed and stood. "Everything." He stepped away, first running his hands through his hair then over his face. "This has been a mess from top to bottom, and the last thing I should have done was take advantage of you."

She wanted to think it was sweet, but the last part irritated her. If she was a different kind of woman, like the kind of women he seemed to work with, he wouldn't feel *guilty*. He just thought she was…fragile. "Well, don't be stupid," she snapped.

"It isn't stupid."

"It is. That kiss wouldn't take advantage of a pig."

"I'm sorry… What?"

"It was a nothing kiss, Holden. I mean, I'm not saying I didn't enjoy it, because I did. Immensely. But it wasn't an advantage when I could have backed away, pushed you off."

"You've been injured. You might have a concussion. I didn't even bandage you up, I just—"

"Oh, shut up. Congratulations. You ruined it. Now, is there a shower in this place? Never mind. I'll find it." And she set out to do just that, letting her anger lead the way.

HOLDEN HAD NO idea what had just happened. He had no idea what had come over him. Just that she was safe and beautiful, but hurt and… He'd just needed to…

It was ridiculous. He'd been out of line. The apology had been the appropriate response, even if it *had* been a nothing kiss.

It hadn't felt like nothing. It felt like being turned inside out. It felt like being absolved of every mistake he'd ever made, and there was no way he could ever be absolved.

He heard the pipes groan. She must have found the shower. Something he wouldn't allow himself to think about too deeply.

There wasn't time to think about anything, except…this assignment that didn't add up. Too many pieces, not enough information, and what little information he had didn't make much sense.

They wanted to take Willa. That was clear. If they had her parents, and were trying to get some kind of information out of them, bringing in Willa would be an incentive for them to spill the beans.

Surely if her parents really were adept spies, though, they'd know whatever information they gave would be the end of all three of their lives.

The sound of water running stopped. Holden braced himself. He had to focus. He had to keep his normal, unbiased, analytical, *intelligent* wits about him. He was going to have to bandage her up and keep his hands to himself. What they both really needed was sleep. They didn't have a ton of time, but a couple hours would put them both on better footing.

Willa waltzed back into the room, wearing nothing but a towel.

"What the hell are you doing?" he demanded. Horrified that he couldn't seem to make himself look away. Her legs were long and toned, a creamy white that must have rarely seen sun. Her arms were tanned and impressively muscled. Her hair was free, an even redder gold when wet with little drops of water trickling from the ends of it over down to the towel. Freckles littered her shoulders and he...

His tongue felt well and truly twisted and stuck in his dry throat.

"Well, I'm not going to put those gross bathroomfight clothes back on now," she said dismissively. She smirked at him. "Do you have anything I could wear?"

He stalked to the closet and pawed around for something that might fit. He tossed a T-shirt and some sweatpants at her.

She began to drop the towel, and he whirled away. Oh no. No, no, no, she was not going to play this game with him. He wouldn't fall for it. "Do you really think now is the time for this?"

"No. I don't. But I get some enjoyment out of you being all huffy and uncomfortable and if you don't find a way to enjoy things even in the toughest circumstances, life can be a real pain."

He happened to agree with her. Or had before he'd taken this job. She'd seemed to take all the humor out of him. She made him feel stiff and uptight. She made him feel like Reece, and that was unacceptable.

He was loose. He was fun. He was *charming*. What kind of spell had she put on him?

Still, he didn't turn to face her. He kept his back to her, his eyes on the ceiling and his thoughts on the fact he had to somehow handle this when he'd never felt so tested in his life.

"Do you have a plan?" she asked. When he didn't

answer, she huffed out a breath. "I'm dressed, you big prude."

He turned around slowly, cautiously. She was indeed dressed and back to sitting on the bed. He crossed over to her, reluctantly taking a bandage from the first aid kit.

He did have a plan. But he hated the plan. Worse, he knew she'd be all about it. Maybe if he talked it out, he could come up with an alternative. Something that didn't involve putting her in any more danger. "Did you hear what the guy was saying?"

"Not really. Something about it not being enough money to kill over?"

"He said it was an open call." With as much space between them as he could manage casually, Holden adhered the bandage to the cut on her temple. "Which is basically where someone sends out a job to the kind of people who do stupid things for money and says they'll pay whoever does the job."

"Like Craigslist for bad guys?"

"Something like that." He held up a finger so she'd sit and wait and went to the kitchen to grab an ice pack. When he returned, he handed it to her, and she put it on her temple without needing the directive to do so.

Her expression was thoughtful. "He had a gun and he didn't shoot me. So the job was, what? Kidnapping me?"

"Seems like." But it didn't add up to the ammunition being sent to Evening. Holden doubted very much if the guy from the bathroom had been the man who'd gotten the ammunition. Now that he'd had time to think it through, the man in the bathroom had been much shorter than the man in the post office video. Also not the brightest or meanest man he'd ever met, which meant he didn't fit for hit man. He was just some moron who liked to get paid for hurting and scaring people.

"What are you thinking?" Willa asked.

"I'm not sure yet. Something doesn't add up here." But he didn't need to tell her all the different ways. Why so cheap if the kidnapping was important? A few thousand bucks wasn't much for an offense with a pretty steep punishment.

"You know what we have to do, Holden. I know you do."

Chapter Fourteen

Willa could see by his expression that he did. He didn't like the idea, obviously. She couldn't say she was too keen on it either, but what other option did they have? She'd checked to make sure her parents hadn't returned her message when she'd been on Holden's phone.

Nothing.

They wouldn't ignore her SOS. They were either continually busy or in serious trouble. There was only one way to get to them.

She watched Holden pace, clearly trying to find another way out of this. She gave him a few minutes to do so. After all, she'd like to do the one where the chances of her ending up dead weren't quite so high.

So, she watched him pace and think from her seat on the bed in the cute little cabin. Was it his? It didn't seem like it. Too utilitarian. It didn't suit him. It probably belonged to his secret group.

She sighed. She was clean, bandaged, wearing no underwear under clothes there were a little too big for her. Holden had kissed her, then acted like seeing her naked would be a personal assault. She refused to let the gravity of the situation undercut her enjoyment of *that*.

"You have to take me to the drop-off, Holden."

He scowled at her. "It's not the only option."

"It is. You have to pretend to be one of these guys who took the job, and succeeded. You could do that, right? Whoever these guys are wouldn't know you work for some group?"

"No, they wouldn't," he said bitterly. "It could be done, but—"

"No buts. That's the plan. You drop me off, like the guy said."

"Then what, Willa? What do you think happens then?"

"They probably take me to my parents and torture me in front of them until my parents tell them what they want to know." She shrugged. She didn't want to think too deeply about the specifics, even though she knew it was something of an inevitability. "But I'd have you."

He looked a little bit like she'd shot him. She was surprised he didn't crumple to the ground.

"I know it's risky, Holden. I understand enough of what my parents do to understand the dangers. But if we work on this together, maybe you could figure out where they are. Or who they are. You and your group could save us."

"Or you could end up dead," he said flatly.

"Yeah. And so could you and my parents and anyone." She knew he wanted her to take this more seriously, but she'd always known this very situation was possible. What and who her parents were had been a shadow over her entire life. Part of why she'd leaned so hard into independence and her own farm was that she'd known her life expectancy could very well be very short.

What she'd never thought possible was help. Someone by her side. Her parents would save her if they could, lay down their lives. She was sure. But Holden could actually *help* her accomplish something. He was her partner now. It gave her an optimism she could only be grateful for.

"You'll drop me off where the guy said," Willa said resolutely. "I don't think my parents will be there, do you?"

"No," he said, an acidic bitterness to the word.

"We'll have to play it by ear, of course. Maybe you let them take me. Maybe you don't. Maybe you follow them. Maybe you bring in your team. I'd trust you to make the right decision in the moment. It really depends on who's there and what the setup is."

He whirled away and began to pace, muttering to himself. There was emotion there. Waves of it. The kind her parents had always warned her about. The kind she'd never been able to fight.

And still, she trusted him to do the right thing. Maybe he'd made a few missteps to his way of thinking—her chaining him to a bed, her fighting off the kidnapper on her own—but he'd handled the kidnapper in a way that never would have occurred to her, getting information out of the guy. They were closer to getting somewhere than she would have been on her own.

"It's the plan you had in mind, isn't it?" she asked gently.

He stopped pacing, and she watched fascinated as he reined all that energy and anger and—she thought maybe—a little fear in. He was cold eyed and tense when he faced her, but not emotional. "Yes," he said through gritted teeth. "That doesn't mean it's the best one."

She smiled at him. "You know it is."

He stood there, still as a mountain. His gaze was blank, but his jaw was tense. He was waging an inner battle. "We need some sleep."

Irritated he wouldn't admit it, she started to get off the bed. "My parents' lives—"

He pushed her gently back onto the mattress. "Willa, you haven't slept for over twenty-four hours, and it's been longer than me. If we're going to face this down—and I'm not so sure we should—the least we need to do to prepare is sleep for a few hours. Not twelve. A few. Brains don't work without sleep."

She knew he was right. She *was* exhausted. But how did she sleep knowing her parents could need her immediate help? How was sleep supposed to solve anything?

She blew out a breath. "For how long?"

He pulled out his phone, tapped the screen. "We'll get four hours. I'm sending a message to my team. They'll scout the area and see what they can figure out before we get there."

She had to suppress a smile. He might *want* there to be another way, but clearly he knew they'd end up doing this. They had to.

"Go to sleep." He started to walk out of the room.

"Whoa, whoa, whoa. Where are you going?"

"To sleep on the couch."

"Yeah, right. You're going to go out there and work. Not gonna fly, buddy. Lie down in here." She patted the bed next to her.

He frowned at the spot but crossed over to it. "Maybe I don't want you taking advantage of me," he said, but he lowered himself onto the bed. With as much room between them on the mattress as possible.

"Of course you do."

He snorted, but he settled his hands over his chest and closed his eyes. She had the sense he went to sleep almost immediately. But as she stared at him, the dark blond lashes against his cheek, the strong jaw she was half tempted to run her fingers across, he turned away from her.

"Go to sleep, Willa," he ordered.

On a sigh, she set out to follow orders.

For now.

HOLDEN SLEPT FOR two hours. It was more than enough with the mixture of worry and adrenaline coursing through him. He eased out of the bed and let Willa continue to sleep.

He pored over the maps Elsie had emailed him, texted with his team as they arrived on-site and started a preliminary sweep of the area. When Shay phoned him, he considered ignoring the call.

He knew she was going to tell him things he didn't want to hear. Worse, he knew he wasn't as in control of himself as he needed to be. Shay would see it. Read into it. *Correctly* read into it.

But he had a job to do, and he wanted his boss on board.

"Hey."

"We got ID on the guy at the gas station. Some penny-ante, low-rate thief. Can't imagine he's much of a threat."

Holden explained what the man had told him. He didn't outline his concerns about things not adding up. Shay would come to that conclusion on her own, and he didn't want Willa trying to eavesdrop if she woke up.

"What's Elsie got?"

"Not much," Shay said. "Computer is pretty encrypted, but she thinks she's making progress."

"Someone needs to be watching her. If there are multiple men trying to kidnap Willa, Elsie isn't safe at that farmhouse alone, even if she is in the bunker."

"She isn't alone."

"I thought you sent my whole team to the wildlife refuge."

"I did, but I called in a favor. You don't worry about Elsie. You worry about how you're going to get to these supposed spies."

"I'm going to have to let them take her, Shay." He

had to say it out loud. He had to hope to God someone had a good reason for him not to do it.

But Shay wasn't that person. "Probably."

Holden bit back an oath. "How am I supposed to
do that?"

"Would you do it if it was me? Or Sabrina? Or any
of us, quite frankly?"

"She's not North Star."

"No, but she's not just any civilian either. Girl's
got chops. Trust her to use them. Then do everything
in your power to make sure it doesn't get her killed."
Shay paused. Meaningfully. "I can send someone
else in if you don't think you're emotionally detached
enough to—"

"I'll handle it. Over and out," Holden muttered, hitting the end button with far too much force. If there
was going to be blood on someone's hands, it was
damn well going to be his own.

He got to his feet. The safe house had an array of
weapons, and he picked what would be best for this
mission. He picked out a few for Willa too. She could
fight like the devil—no doubt her parents had trained
her in how to shoot a gun as well.

Then he pushed away his guilt at pawing through
her things and found the papers she'd been trying to
make sense of before the gas station stop.

The code was complex, and he spent far too long
trying to beat his head against it before his phone
alarm went off, telling him to wake up Willa.

When he woke Willa up after her four hours of

sleep, he foisted a sandwich on her. "Wake up. Eat. We leave in fifteen."

She blinked at him, sleep clouding her eyes. "Dream you was much nicer," she muttered.

He didn't let himself dwell on *that* comment. He left the sandwich on the nightstand and went back to getting ready. When she emerged from the room a few minutes later, she was pulling at the shirt she was wearing.

"I can't wear this."

The T-shirt was white and dangerously close to see-through. The sweatpants were baggy and loose. Holden wrenched his gaze away and went to the mudroom. He pulled her clothes out of the dryer then returned to the main room and handed them to her. "Washed and dried."

"Well, aren't you handy."

"Something like that."

She frowned at her own clothes, clean and warm from the dryer. "Did you sleep? You were supposed to sleep."

"I slept. Just not the full four hours. I had plans to make. Now, we need to go. We don't want to wait till dark. Get dressed, and eat that sandwich."

She grumbled but did as she was told. She still had shadows under her eyes, bruising that made his stomach clench into nasty knots. But she was awake and alert and...

Hell, he didn't know how he was going to do this. Only that he had to.

When she returned, they loaded up the car in silence. Holden didn't tell her the plan or where they were going. She didn't ask. She pored over her papers.

"Any luck?"

"Not really. Part of me wonders if it's…purposeful. Too hard for me to crack so I can't help them."

"I don't know anything about cracking codes, but I've got one of my men on it."

She frowned over at him. "Huh?"

"I sent a picture over. We don't have any code experts right now, but we have a few people with those kinds of brains."

"I didn't say you could do that."

"Are we on the same team or not, Willa?"

"We are, but these are codes my parents put together. This was for me. For me alone."

He couldn't say she sounded angry. Maybe closer to betrayed. Which he could hardly let bother him. "I have a job to do, Willa."

"Yes. I'm very well aware. I shouldn't have…" She shook her head and blew out a breath. There was *still* something she wasn't telling him.

It, along with his own ridiculous reactions, grated. The whole thing grated. He flicked a glance at her. She'd stopped looking at the code and stared very hard out the window. She twisted her fingers together, clearly lost in her own secretive thoughts.

"Sometimes I don't know if I'm doing the right thing," she said very quietly, and the sadness in her tone had that frustration twining into something closer to guilt.

"No one ever knows if they're doing the right thing, Willa. We just do our best guess."

She shook her head. "I just don't know if they would have wanted me to take that code. They gave me no clear SOS. It's just, I didn't think they ever would. Maybe I should have left it. Maybe I'm making things worse."

She was nervous. *He* was nervous. Which was fine. Nerves weren't something to conquer. They were something to control. He supposed any other emotions plaguing him at the moment were the same. He'd accept them.

He'd control them.

"We can't second-guess at this point, Willa. We have to move forward, armed with the information we have. I have a team in place, but they have to stay pretty far back to avoid detection. They won't intervene unless I give them the signal. Mostly, I want them there so if we do have to let these guys take you, I have more than just myself following the trail."

"But what if the guys suspect something?"

"One of two potential outcomes. One, they close up shop and head back to wherever they're headquartered. Not a bad option because we can follow them that way too."

"The other option is bloody shoot-out?"

Holden spared her a look. "They might try the offensive, but I have five guys on the area. From all my scouts, they've only got three."

"Three?"

"It's just a drop-off."

"A few thousand dollars. A few men. I can't say I feel all that important."

It was the part that grated. It was the part that didn't add up. Still, Holden kept his shrug nonchalant. "Maybe they don't expect you to put up much of a fight. Maybe you *aren't* that important." He wished he could believe it. "Maybe you're…an insurance policy. They have a different plan in place, but they'll use you if you have to."

She frowned at him. "Why do I get the sneaking suspicion you have a completely different and much more terrifying hypothesis?"

Chapter Fifteen

His eyes stayed on the road, but she could have sworn his grip on the steering wheel tightened.

Fear drummed in Willa's throat, but she breathed through it carefully. It was all scary, but panic wouldn't solve anything.

"Holden."

"I don't have a more terrifying hypothesis. I don't have a hypothesis. But I don't like when things don't add up. You not being worth more attention doesn't fully add up." The car slowed. "But we don't have time to figure it out, because here we go."

She saw the sign for the wildlife refuge, and her heart thudded hard against her ribs, the beating seeming to echo in her ears. *Here we go.*

After they entered, Holden slowed to a stop next to a big sign that had a map of the area plastered on it.

"Lake three," he said, reaching through his rolled-down window and tapping the map. "This one right here. I want you to get a picture of this map in your head. If you have to run, you run north or south." He pointed to both directions on the map. "I've got men on either side there. One grabs you, he'll say, 'North Star.' That's the cue to let them take you wherever. They're safe. I've got east and west points, too, but they're farther out. So north or south. That's all you have to remember. I tell you to run—"

"I run north or south. I got it. Holden, what if this code tells us something important? Or to stay away? Or…"

"Do you want to backtrack? We can go wait in that cabin if you want, Willa. We'd be safe there. We can take the time to figure out the code."

She could tell he wanted her to agree. She knew she couldn't. In order for this to look like Holden really had her, he had to bring her today. Much more time and whoever had her parents would surely suspect this whole thing. She shook her head. "As long as they might be in danger…"

He gave a sharp nod, then started driving again.

"When we see the signal, I'm going to get out of the car slowly and carefully. I have weapons in the backpack I'll wear, but they'll search me probably. That's okay, I've got more in the car. The most important thing is to stay calm and let them do as much talking as possible."

Willa nodded. She tried not to look as terrified as she felt. She needed him to believe she was capable of this. That they were equal partners.

"I'm going to have to shake you around a bit, and when I do, that's when you start the waterworks, okay? Act like you're scared and I've roughed you up. We want them to think you're as weak as possible. The more they underestimate you, the better off we are."

Willa nodded. It centered her, oddly. She could act as scared as she felt, and it would only work in their favor.

"It is my last resort option to leave you with them. Understand that. If we have to go that route, you'll have six highly trained field operatives following you. I won't let anything happen to you."

It was probably foolish to think him saying *I* over *we* meant something, but she could be foolish in her own mind. Especially now.

They pulled up to the sign for lake three. There was a lone fisherman standing at the lake. He held a pole but wasn't dressed for fishing. He was smoking a cigarette, and even though the jacket he wore concealed everything, even Willa could tell he was armed to the hilt.

"I'm going to get out. You stay in until I come get you. Remember, if you have to run, it's north or south. North Star is your safety net."

Willa nodded. She didn't trust her voice or, more, her expression now that the fisherman was watching them.

"Don't move."

Holden slid out of the car, and Willa could only sit in the passenger side seat, watching. Holden had his back to her, but she could see the fisherman as he turned to Holden.

Holden must have said something to go along with the wide hand gesture he made. The man flicked his cigarette into the lake. His eyes were dark and hard. He had a scar under one eye, a nose that listed to the left and a missing bottom tooth. He looked every part the bad guy.

Willa wished that could comfort her in some way. But so many things didn't add up, and she didn't know how to wait until they did.

She looked down at the code in her lap. She'd figured out one part, but it didn't make any sense on its own. Industries. That could be anything. It was a name. Something Industries. And she thought maybe the last word was *warehouse*.

A warehouse for something called… Maybe Ross Industries. She wished she could search in her phone, but she knew anyone could be watching her, and they'd think it irregular enough she was sitting here unrestrained.

Had Holden thought that through? Surely he knew better than to… He started stalking back toward the car. She couldn't read his expression, didn't know if it was real or a mask. He opened the car door and didn't waste time, didn't say anything.

He took her by the arm and pulled her out of the car. She pretended to try to shake off his grasp.

"You're sure lucky they wanted you in one piece, sweetheart," Holden said, pushing her forward with more theatrics than force. He took her to the fisherman, who'd since dropped his pole.

"What's your name?" the man demanded.

"None of your business," Willa retorted, but her voice shook, and she looked at the sun, rather than the man, which helped her eyes water effectively. "I don't know who you are or what you want, but you've made a mistake and you need to let me go."

"Or what?" Holden said with a nasty laugh.

She knew he was playing a part, but that didn't make it comfortable how well he fell into the role of sleazy bad guy.

"We need some proof you brought us the right package," the man said. He held up a hand, and a man materialized out of the woods surrounding the lake. Willa didn't have to feign fear. This man had his weapons strapped across his body like armor.

Like a very valid threat.

"Well, you don't need me for this part," Holden said, and he licked his lips and looked around nervously. He even loosened his grasp on her arm. "Just hand over the fee and I'll be out of your hair."

"Can't pay you until we have confirmation," the man replied, and his cold stare never left Willa. The other man came over to him, carrying something. He handed it over to the fisherman.

It was some kind of cloth. It looked a bit like the handkerchiefs her father liked to carry. The cold shudder of trepidation turned into an icy ball of fear as the man pulled a pair of glasses out of the handkerchief.

Willa let out a gasp, one she didn't have to feign. It could be coincidence, but clearly they wanted her to, at the very least, think they had her father. At the very worst, they knew enough about her father to replicate the things he would have carried on him. "Those are my father's. Where did you get that?"

He nodded at the second man. "Excuse us." Both men turned their backs on Willa and Holden. Willa wanted to run. Away, to save herself. At them, to get her father's belongings. But all she could do was stand next to this lake and breathe too hard, furiously fighting the tears that wanted to fall.

Someone *did* have her parents, and now they wanted her.

Suddenly Holden was close. Too close, his mouth practically brushing her ear. "The minute the third guy comes out of the trees..." Holden muttered so quietly she almost couldn't hear him. "Fight for your life." Then he slid the handle of a knife into her hand.

HOLDEN HAD NO better grasp of what they were getting into, but he could see clearly based on how the men were positioned, what weapons they had and what vehicles they didn't, that this wasn't supposed to end with either him or Willa making it out alive.

He'd made out two men in the woods straight off, though he knew he wasn't supposed to. He was *supposed* to be a penny-ante thief who wouldn't think to look for complications.

The hidden men were complications. Even when the one came out to "confirm" Willa's identification.

This was no kidnapping drop-off. Maybe they were only planning on killing him so he couldn't talk to anyone about the package he'd dropped off, but why make an open call then? That in and of itself left a trail.

It was possible, more than possible, that something

had changed with Willa's parents. Either they already gave the information they were supposed to keep secret, or they'd already been eliminated —which made Willa the loose end that needed tying. It could even be they'd escaped, and Willa's head was going to be the payback. But the fact they had Willa's father's belongings had Holden, unfortunately, leaning toward them already being dead.

But still. Too many possibilities. Too many options. Holden wasn't about to let either of them be heads on a platter. Maybe she'd never forgive him if he prioritized her life over her parents' lives, but she was the life he had in his hands. Hers was the life he had to save.

He wanted to give her a gun, but it would take more time to get one out of the pack, so the knife he'd been able to conceal in his belt would have to do.

His team would come running once he shot his gun, but that had to be done at the right moment. When he and Willa weren't so close to the men here, who had much more powerful and lethal guns than he had access to at the moment.

There was also the possibility these three men had their own team waiting, though it would have to be much farther away than his if his team hadn't caught wind of them in their survey of the area.

The two men by the lake came back to them. "Come with us," the fisherman said, pointing toward the woods.

Holden gave it one last chance. "You don't need me anymore. Just hand over the cash and I disappear."

The man from the woods shook his head, but he didn't speak. He grabbed Willa's arm and started pulling her toward the woods, the fisherman doing the same to Holden.

Holden didn't fight back yet. He let himself be dragged, though he put up a bit of a fight. Worked on looking scared instead of ready to fight for his life.

The third man stepped out of the woods and Holden watched, waited, calculated. Once they were within reach, he dug in his heels. "Now," Holden said firmly.

He landed an elbow into the taller man's nose with his free arm, then used his backpack as a weapon, flinging it off his back and at the new shooter. He didn't expect to hurt him, just wanted to knock the gun away for the extra seconds it would take for Holden to tackle him to the ground.

It felt a little bit too much like slow motion, because as the pack hit the gun, causing the gunman to jerk with the force, Holden had to trust Willa to fight off the third.

Until he could get to a gun and fire off a warning shot, his team would not advance.

Holden dived, knocking into the third shooter. It was easy then to land a few key punches and rip the high-powered weapon out of the man's hands.

He picked off the fisherman, who instead of going after him had turned his attentions to Willa. She'd clearly managed to knock both men off her, keeping them too busy dodging blows to shoot. If they were going to. Holden still wasn't completely convinced they were meant to kill Willa, but they certainly weren't afraid to hurt her.

Holden couldn't shoot the man she was currently grappling with because he could too easily hit her— no matter how good a shot he was, they were moving too much. So he had to throw himself into the fray.

He dived in and landed a punch, but got the wind knocked out of him by the man's elbow. Willa got a nasty shin kick in, but the man took her by the hair and threw her to the ground, raising his gun to point at Holden. Holden pushed him and grabbed him by the shirtfront, ready to use his own badly bruised head as a weapon, but out of the corner of his eye, Holden saw the man he'd knocked to the ground lift his arm. He ignored the one pointed at his heart and shot the guy on the ground who was still trying to shoot Willa.

Kill Willa.

For what? Why was she the target when she hadn't been a day ago?

Holden braced for the bullet that was no doubt coming for him. But when the shot rang out, just as he was attempting to jump out of the way, he felt nothing.

The man he'd been holding crumpled to the ground. It took Holden a second or two to let him go. To look up and see Gabriel, gun in hand, standing at the edge of the woods.

"Saved by the sniper," he muttered to himself, turning to find Willa. She was splattered with blood, but most of it wasn't hers. Thank God.

The North Star team began to tighten their circle around the nasty scene. One member to each immobilized or dead man. Gabriel came up to Holden, grim faced and serious. "We were moving in before your shot. We got an urgent message from Shay to move in."

"Why?"

Gabriel shrugged. "Wasn't given the details. Just told to get you guys out."

Holden frowned at that. It wasn't like Shay not to lay the whole picture on the line. She didn't like her operatives acting without knowing all the details, all the whys and all the possible outcomes. "You got your phone?" Holden had left his in the car, knowing he didn't want any of the men he'd originally been meeting to get a handle on North Star property.

Gabriel handed his over. Holden went through the complicated process of patching through to Shay.

"Saunders?"

"What's going on?" Holden demanded.

He heard Shay sigh. But when she spoke, it was all authoritative demand. "Report on the situation at hand, Holden."

"We fought them off, then my team saved my butt. What's going on that you sent them early and not on my signal?" Thank God she had, but that didn't ease the discomfort in his gut that something was very, very wrong.

"That code Willa's parents left her? It isn't just a location, or information about who they're working for or why. If our code breaker is right, they gave her evidence on an entire arm of the organization the feds are after. An organization that'll do anything to make sure it doesn't get into the feds' hands."

Chapter Sixteen

Willa watched as Holden's expression went completely lax. His surprise terrified her more than fighting off men with guns. What could surprise Holden at this point?

"We've got to get out of here," Holden said, taking her arm. And giving her absolutely no comfort whatsoever. He tossed the phone back at his team member without a second glance.

"But—"

He shook his head, issuing orders to the members of his team. They'd take care of the mess, no doubt, but Holden was leading her to the car. Getting out of here. When none of this had gone to plan.

"Hold—"

"I'll explain everything when we're back at the safe house. I promise."

But he sounded gutted. A little horrified. "Is it my parents?" she asked, feeling light-headed. Some mix of adrenaline wearing off and utter terror that he'd gotten news her parents were dead and none of this mattered anymore.

"No. No word on your parents," he said, and his hold on her gentled as he opened the passenger side door.

She let out a relieved breath and all but melted into the seat. But there was a tension, a worry in him as he walked around the front of the car, and she couldn't help but feel both seep into her bones.

If they hadn't had word on her parents, what was so bad? That they'd been willing to kill her?

She'd had a decent amount of certainty the men had wanted her alive, until Holden had said *now* as they'd reached the third man. There'd been something about the look that man had given her, the way the gun was pointed at her, that made her believe they meant to kill her. Then and there.

Why would they want her alive in one breath, and dead in another?

Holden didn't drive fast this time. No, the pace was well within the speed limit, his gaze was steady on the road, and even when they turned off onto the unmarked path to the cabin, he kept his silence.

The silence felt oppressive, but Willa didn't know what to say to break it. She should demand answers, but she was terrified of them.

They'd come anyway. Whether she asked or not.

Holden stopped the car in front of the cabin they'd been in. Had it only been a few hours ago? It was full on dark now, and Willa wished she was home with her animals. But there was starlight and moonlight and...

She glanced over at Holden as she followed him to the door. Something was going on. Something he didn't know how to work out. She figured a man like Holden wanted to figure it out before he told her.

There was no time for that. If these men suddenly wanted her dead, then the chances of her parents living through this grew slimmer and slimmer with every minute.

They stepped inside, and Holden locked the door behind her. He set a security code, and though he didn't make a full tour of the cabin, she could tell his eyes swept everything, making sure no one had come in while they'd been gone.

"We should change our bandages," he said, and she had to assume he saw nothing suspicious. "Ice everything down. Get a meal in. Then sleep. We both need to sleep." He moved for the kitchen.

Willa didn't scoff or argue. She simply stood in the middle of the living room and stared at him. Waiting.

He grabbed an ice pack out of the freezer and turned to face her.

"You'll explain that phone call to me now," she said, sounding calm and measured. She wasn't sure how. She felt a lot like sinking to the floor and crying.

But there was no time.

Holden sighed and dropped the ice pack on the counter, then scrubbed his hands over his face. "It was Shay. About the codes your parents gave you. It isn't just whereabouts or even the name of who they're working for."

Willa shook her head. "I know there's a lot on the papers, but they include a lot of decoy information so that—"

"My team broke the code, Willa. We know what it says. It's evidence. Evidence against a very dangerous organization. They know you have it or have access to it. That's why they wanted you alive."

"But then they didn't."

"I know. Something happened. Something changed. They wanted you dead."

Willa absorbed that blow, but it didn't take long. Her wheels were already turning. Because something had changed and it wasn't her or Holden, but she didn't know a darn thing about Holden's group.

For a while there, whoever had her parents had only wanted to kidnap her. They could have killed her back at the farmhouse, but they'd tried to kill Holden. The job that had been set out for two-bit criminals had been to take her, alive, to the drop-off location.

Something changed. His group had the information her parents had left her for emergencies only. "This group didn't always know I had access to evidence. Neither of us knew we had evidence. Right here. With us."

Holden's eyebrows drew together. "What does that mean?"

"It means they didn't know I had a code, which includes even more important information than I thought, until you sent pictures to your team. Up until that meet up at the lake, they only wanted to take me. They didn't want me dead."

If he hadn't put that information together, he didn't show surprise, and yet something in him changed—

she couldn't have said what. Only that it made her... uneasy. On top of scared and suspicious.

"My team isn't dirty, if that's what you're saying."

"I wouldn't know, Holden. I don't know anything about them. Why should I trust them? Why should I trust..." She didn't finish the sentence, because it was ridiculous to question trusting him at this point. She did, whether she'd wanted to or not, and they'd worked together to save each other's lives more than once at this point.

"Go ahead and say it," Holden said flatly.

Temper started to mount, mixing with fear. She knew irrational outbursts could only follow, but how much was a woman supposed to just *take*? "I wish I could say it! I wish I could mean it! But I trust you. With my life, turns out. So don't get all testy on me. Someone in your team had to have done *something* that allowed this bad group..." The group. If the code had a name or a whereabout, they had a lead on where her parents were. "The group—does the code say who they are?"

"You sure change channels fast," he muttered.

"My parents' lives are at stake. I don't have time to be angry or fight with you about whether your team is dirty or not. I *have* to get to them before they're killed. I have to."

Holden blew out a breath. "Let's call Shay."

It ate at him. Even as Shay explained to both him and Willa on speakerphone that the group who likely had Willa's parents was called Ross Industries, which was obviously a front for something else. Elsie was working on that, but carefully. Elsie confirmed that there was no way her searching had led anyone to know they or Willa had evidence against them.

"I know you want to move on your parents, Willa," Shay was saying in her calm, authoritative tone. "Trust me, I know. But if we have any hope for avoiding loss of life, I need some time. We'll send an entire team in."

Willa sat on the couch. Hands clutched together on her lap. "Is there any way you can guarantee my parents are still alive?"

There was a pause. One far too long.

"I can't at the moment," Shay admitted. "But I will do everything in my power to get you some kind of answer in the next few hours. Okay?"

It was more than Holden had expected out of Shay, but he'd forgotten in the two years of Shay's leadership role that she'd once been a person who rarely went by the book—even North Star's.

"Thank you. Thank you. I…" Willa trailed off and looked up at him, some inner debate warring in her expression. "If you can use me as some kind of bait or trade or whatever, I want you to."

"Willa—"

"No, don't argue with me," Willa said, cutting off Shay's protests. But her eyes remained on him as she spoke. "I want you to promise me, if I can help, you'll send me. I need you to. They're my parents. I have to do everything in my power to save them. I'd like to do it with your help, but if you can't promise me that, I walk."

"It's a little hard to walk when I've got an agent on you."

"I walk," Willa repeated firmly. To Shay. To him.

Holden could stop her from walking. He could stop her from doing a lot of things.

But he knew he wouldn't. He understood too well what a child would need to sacrifice to save their parents. He couldn't stop the car crash that had taken his father before he'd been born. He couldn't stop the cancer that had taken his mother far too young.

If he had the opportunity to give Willa the chance to save her parents, he would. He had to.

Somehow, she understood that. Or at least guessed at it. Or maybe she just underestimated his ability to keep her prisoner if he wanted to. But he had the sneaking suspicion she just…understood him.

A problem, that.

"Stay in the safe house for now. Let me get men on the ground at this warehouse, a good sweep and some intel. We'll update you in the morning, and the minute I get confirmation on your parents, I'll pass it along to Holden. But for tonight, I want you two staying put. It's part of our job to keep you safe as well, Willa. Not just your parents."

"I know it's silly, but—"

"Your animals are in good hands. We've got three people here at your house, and between the three of us and some internet searching, we've been taking pretty good care of all of them. We'll do our best to continue to."

"I appreciate it," Willa said, though Holden didn't think she sounded all that sincere.

He picked up the phone, clicked the speaker off. "We'll hold tight. You've got someone with Elsie, right? If they're looking for information, it's not unreasonable to think they might return to the farmhouse."

"I'm here. So is Granger."

Holden nearly bobbled his phone. "Granger?" Holden couldn't check his surprise at Shay involving their old boss.

"Came kicking and screaming, but I told him we were spread thin and he didn't want Elsie caught in the crossfire, did he?"

"Fight dirty."

"When it suits. Keep your target there under control. Holden, if I find out her parents are dead, I'm not passing that along until this is over."

Holden closed his eyes. He wished Shay hadn't told him that. Still, he gave her a quiet affirmation before hanging up the phone.

Willa was still sitting on the couch, her hands folded together. She was deep in thought, and every once in a while she leaned forward and wrote something down on a scratch pad of paper. Then she'd sit back, link her fingers and think again.

Holden should do something. Eat. Sleep. Figure out what the hell was going on with this Ross Industries. But all he could seem to do was watch her.

"What are you writing down?"

"A list. A list of things we need to do. *I* need to do. I realize your group is on it, but I need to be doing something, too. I'm sorry, I don't trust your group. Not enough."

"Willa."

"No, I'm sorry. Shay said something to you after you were off speaker. You don't want to tell me, fine. But secrets are secrets, and I don't trust that. I won't." She stood, holding her piece of paper. "First, I want you to get the address to that warehouse."

"Willa. They didn't give it to me for a reason. It might not even be where your parents are."

She waved that away. "We don't need to use it, per se. I just want you to have it. In case we need it. I want you to have it as backup. Can you do that?"

"Can? Yeah. Will I?"

She kept speaking as if the answer to that question was an obvious yes. "We'll wait here tonight. I agree with that. We'll need the intel your group finds before we make any moves. If someone in your group is dirty—"

"North Star isn't dirty," he interrupted. But she'd planted a doubt earlier. It had happened, now and again, when they'd tried to take down the Sons. Someone would be compelled to step over that line. Hell, the explosion they'd had two years ago had been due to Granger trusting the wrong double agent.

She looked up at him, stern as a schoolteacher. "You're letting your emotions cloud reality, Holden."

"No, I'm letting facts and experience and my gut

influence my decision making, as it should be. First of all, we don't know *what's* going on with this Ross Industries. The change from kidnapping to murder could have to do with *anything*." Including the death of her parents, but he wouldn't say that to her. He couldn't.

So, he continued on *his* point. "It's not Shay. I know that. Down to my soul, I know it's not Shay or Elsie. You'd have to meet Elsie and you'd see it too. She's…good. The bone-deep kind you don't see all that often. The five we had out with us this afternoon? Apart from trusting them with my life for years, it doesn't make sense. They came in and saved my butt. They could have let them take us. They didn't. I'm not saying there's not something…more here. A computer hack? Someone saying the wrong thing to the wrong person. But I don't see a leak. Not a purposeful one. It can't be. I know these people. I trust these people."

She blinked up at him, her expression softening into something he didn't trust. Not for the life of him.

"They're like your family," she said softly.

He stepped back as if she'd struck him. Something worked through him, and he didn't know the emotion, so he tried to convince himself it was offense. "I can do my job impartially."

"No. No, that isn't what I mean." She moved over to him and reached her hand up to touch his face. "You don't have to *be* a job, Holden. When it's people you love, it isn't so easy to *be* the job anymore. You're family. You care. I don't mean you can't do your job, partially or impartially. I mean, you *care*."

He took her arm by the wrist and pulled her hand off his face. "I don't think you understand."

"I do. I grew up with my parents doing what you're doing. They loved each other. I may not have understood everything they did or went through, but I could watch and guess. You care about your team, so it's complicated. I care about my parents, so it's complicated." She blew out a breath, and it was only as she made a move to walk away from him that he realized he'd kept his grip on her wrist.

She seemed to realize it then, too. She looked first at his hand holding her, then up at him. There wasn't questioning in her gaze so much as consideration. She didn't pull away. If anything she drifted closer.

It was all her talk about care and complications, and the truth here. With her hand in his, with her green eyes on his. Not just his team, who *had* become his family. But her. Who'd somehow become... something. "I care, so it's complicated," he said. For himself. About her. Though he should have shut his idiotic mouth.

He should have left it at that. He should have walked away. Gotten to work, because even if they were staying put for the night, surely there was still work to do. But he didn't let go of her hand, and when she rose on her tiptoes, he didn't push away.

He let her kiss him, and he kissed her back.

Chapter Seventeen

It wasn't like when Holden had kissed her earlier today. Had that been today? Had it only been days since she'd known him? Willa felt like she understood everything about him. She felt like he was a part of her life. Inextricably.

No doubt she'd feel differently once this burned out. She might even regret it. But for now she wanted to feel something other than lost. Something other than alone.

Because she wasn't alone. Maybe it was only for a short while, but she had him, and his kiss lit her from the inside out. It wasn't gentle or tentative. If he had regrets, he was saving them for later.

She wrapped her arms around his neck and poured everything she was into the kiss. If she had to stay here and let someone else take the reins to her and her parents' lives, why not take something for herself? Mistakes felt a lot less scary when life or death hung in the balance not too far away.

Holden's arms were strong and tight around her. His body hard, sturdy against hers. His mouth was an anchor to something new. Something bright and wonderful and *connected*. His teeth scraped against her bottom lip, and she felt alive. Well and truly linked. Not just to some random guy, or even the guy who'd helped her, fought side by side with her.

But the man who'd talked to her about his family, who'd bandaged her cuts gently because he cared that she'd been hurt. He'd spoke of one of his teammates as bone-deep good, and so was he.

She understood he thought himself as bad because he'd gotten mixed up in something bad once when he'd been a teenager and grieving, but he wasn't. He was good and noble, and his need to set things to rights made her care about him as much as this attraction did.

She knew she'd never be able to explain that to him in words, so she tried to explain it to him in feelings.

Everything gentled. Imperceptibly almost, but her knees felt weak as his hands cupped her face. Heat was intoxicating. It dulled thought and reason. Gentleness went deeper. It was the promise of something more than what they had. It gave her hope. One that wasn't particularly comfortable.

But she'd never been after comfort.

Holden tore his mouth from hers. "I can't do this," he said, his voice rough and low.

But he was breathing hard and still holding her tight. His words didn't match his actions. At *all*.

"Why not?"

"It isn't right."

"Why not?"

He gave her one of those disapproving looks, and though he started trying to put distance between them, she wouldn't let him.

"Well, why not, Holden?"

"Stop saying why not," he ordered, trying to pull her arms off his neck. But she simply wouldn't let him.

"Then give me a good answer."

"We're in the middle of something dangerous. You're worried about your parents. You've somehow planted worries in my head about my own team."

She heard excuses more than reasons. Because even if the reasons were true, they paled in comparison to this. "But you care. And I care."

"Willa…"

She would miss the way he said her name in exasperation. The loss of it would feel insurmountable if she wasn't also facing the loss of her parents, or even her own life. Maybe she'd die trying to save her parents. She would if she had to.

She didn't want to die without this moment. It would be a waste. "I know in a few hours it all changes. Trust me, I know. But I also know… You have to take what you can get. Even when it's not perfect. That's what my life taught me. Nothing's ever going to be perfect, so you reach for all you can."

"Maybe I don't want to reach because I know what it feels like to lose."

"Oh, Holden." It just about broke her heart in two. Maybe she should trust him. He'd suffered losses far more significant than she ever had. But she couldn't understand shutting herself down because of what *might* come. And much like she'd never wanted to be a spy like her parents because she wanted free rein over her emotions, she didn't want to control her emotions now. She wanted it all. "Feelings aren't win or lose. Not these."

She'd never convince him of that with words, so she kissed him again, hoping to find a way past all those protections. All those walls. He deserved more than the little prison he'd made for himself. He'd let his group become his family, though he hadn't admitted it to himself yet, but he was still so often separate from them.

She understood that, too, even if her loneliness was somewhat self-imposed. Or necessary. Or *whatever*. For a few hours, she had license to be *with* someone. To give herself over to the opposite of loneliness, to connection and care.

He lifted her off her feet, and she laughed against his mouth. It felt good to laugh. To pause everything. There was nothing else to be done, so why not find solace in something that wasn't bleak at all?

He carried her into the bedroom, his mouth never leaving hers. She held on tight, wanting the moment to last, wanting to rush ahead. Wanting anything and everything from him. She tugged at his shirt and he deposited her on the bed, then pulled it off himself.

He was pure rangy muscle, and Willa's stomach and heart jumped in time—attraction, and something that felt a little deeper than the word *care* she kept using.

She reached out and smoothed her palm over the splotching of scars on his side. "What happened?"

He knelt on the bed next to her, then tugged at her shirt until she lifted her arms and let him take it off her. "Explosions."

"Plural?"

He shrugged. A careless yes.

But it wasn't careless. He'd been marred and marked by the work he'd chosen to do. To make something right. She kissed the white line on his shoulder. "And this one?"

"Knife. Got that one trying to escape the gang I'd gotten myself mixed up in."

Gotten himself. Hardly. To her way of thinking, anyone who'd gotten him involved in a gang had manipulated him and used his grief against him. But he wouldn't appreciate her theory, so she kept her mouth shut.

She pointed at the scar on his side, still pink as though the injury hadn't been all that long ago. "That one?"

He looked down as if he didn't even know his own scars. He shrugged again. "Shot."

He laid her back on the bed, his hands trailing down her sides. He unbuttoned her pants, slid them over her hips and off. She was in her underwear, with a *man*, and she didn't feel self-conscious. She felt... Well, the way he looked at her made her beautiful. Her skin practically *hummed*.

"Do you want to keep talking about my scars?" he asked, looking down at her with a smug smile.

"Maybe," she offered, making a motion that he should take his own pants off as she sat up.

He grinned and dropped them. There was a jagged line on his thigh. She simply raised an eyebrow.

He looked down at it, as if he didn't even remember it was there. "Oh. Sabrina and a broken bottle."

"Who's Sabrina?"

"Another agent."

"She hurt you with a broken bottle?" Willa asked, unable to keep the outrage out of her voice.

"It was before she was an agent. We got in a bar fight."

Willa didn't know *what* to make of that, but she found she didn't like the name Sabrina. Or the way Holden sounded almost proud she'd wounded him with a broken bottle, for heaven's sake. "Is she pretty?"

Holden laughed. "I guess so."

"What does *that* mean?"

"She's more like my little sister than anything else." He pressed a kiss to her neck, one that had heat shuddering through her like a storm. "Want to ask me any more questions?"

"Hmm. Oh." She slid her fingers through the hair at his temples, liking the slightly coarse texture, so much different than her hair. "Who patches you up when you're hurt in the line of duty?"

"Betty. She's our doctor." He nibbled down her shoulder, and she found she liked that as much as she liked him answering her questions without stiffening up.

"You really are a little family, aren't you?" she murmured, kissing his jaw.

He rolled her onto her back, pinning her to the mattress. It was meant to be playful, to change the subject. He was even smiling, but it faded. Slowly. She wasn't sure it was doubt causing him to sober, so much as... fear.

"I want you, Holden," she said, trying to match his smile, but there was such seriousness in him. "That's all that matters for a little bit. I want you."

HOLDEN COULDN'T REMEMBER the last time he'd been so relaxed. Though he had always worked hard to put off a careless air, there'd always been a center of…well, whatever made a man get involved with a gang, then leave it for a secretive group that worked tirelessly for years to take down that gang.

He tried to remind himself it was wrong. A man like him letting a woman like Willa curl up next to him, head on his shoulder, hand curled over his heart.

"You should have told me I was your first," he murmured, trying to work up some kind of moral outrage on her behalf. But he was having a hard time keeping his eyes open, and mostly he wanted to press his nose into her hair and fall asleep.

She yawned. "Why?"

"I…" He wasn't sure he could articulate why. She was too sweet, too responsive to do anything but take his time. Linger. It had been…beyond what he'd known this kind of thing could be.

It should have scared him, but he hadn't worked up to that yet.

She was beautiful. He wanted her. Not just in the moment. He wanted her in his life. The way she went toe to toe to him. The way she understood him in ways he wasn't altogether certain he understood himself. Or maybe she just put words to things he tried not to.

It wasn't done. It wasn't possible. Maybe Reece had gone down that particular road, but this was different. Holden wasn't Reece.

Besides, it was clear to Holden—or at least he was trying to make it clear to himself in the aftermath— she knew she was going into a dangerous situation, one she thought she might not come out of on the other side. So, she'd had some kind of last hurrah.

Well, that was fine and dandy, but she needed to be clear about one thing. "You're not going to die. That isn't going to happen."

She eased up onto her elbow, looking down at him. Her hair had mostly fallen out of its band and was a curling mass around her shoulders. She looked fresh faced, satisfied and so damn beautiful it *hurt*.

The expression of confusion melted slowly into one of understanding. Why did she always seem to understand him?

"I didn't have sex with you as some kind of virginal last hurrah before I plan on dying, Holden."

Since he felt scolded, he shrugged and tried to act nonchalant. "I didn't say you did."

"But you thought it." She gave him a quick peck

on the mouth. "I'm starving." She slid out of bed, grabbed his T-shirt and slid it over her head. "Is there food in that kitchen?"

"Yeah." He got out of bed, too, pulling on his jeans. He didn't feel like pawing through the community clothes to find a shirt that would fit him, so he followed Willa into the kitchen.

She hummed to herself, and though she clearly didn't know where anything in the kitchen was, she poked through cabinets and drawers with the quiet confidence of someone who might have lived here.

"You're smug," he grumbled.

"I am. Quite smug." She grinned at him. Her hair hid most of her bandage, but Holden could see she'd bled through. "You need that bandage changed."

She glanced over at him. "Right back at you."

He muttered to himself as he collected the first aid supplies, and though he was trying to act grumpy or harsh, he didn't feel any of it. The whole thing felt so right, so comfortable, he couldn't seem to muster up the necessary self-loathing or situational irritation.

Must be the lack of sleep. And food. He'd think straight once they ate and slept.

She had a peanut butter sandwich made when he returned, laying all the supplies out on the counter. He motioned her to come closer, and she did.

She offered him the sandwich, but since his hands were full, he just leaned forward and took a bite. Then he went about changing out her bandage while she ate.

Then they switched, him finishing off the sandwich and her rebandaging his head.

"Matching head wounds," she said with a smile, smoothing the adhesive gently into place.

"Yeah, the difference is you gave me this one and then chained me to a bed."

She laughed, and the hand that had put on the bandage smoothed over his cheek, then rested there. There was something in her eyes. Something he intellectually knew he wasn't ready for, but his heart seemed to be galloping ahead without heeding any reality.

"Willa…" He couldn't say it. He couldn't *mean* it. Thank *God* his phone went off.

He grabbed it like a lifeline, moving away from her soft touch and softer eyes. Glancing at the phone screen he saw that it was Shay. "Parker," he greeted. He heard the distinct sound of gunfire and glass shattering. He didn't bother to ask what was going on. "I'm on my way."

"Bring her," Shay demanded. "We might need her. Approach with caution."

Then the line went dead. Holden held the phone for one second in shock, but then immediately pushed himself out of it.

"Get dressed," he ordered. "We have to get to your farmhouse."

"What's going on?" she asked, but she was already moving for the bedroom and their clothes.

"I'm not sure." But it was bad. Very bad.

Chapter Eighteen

Willa's heart felt as though it was permanently lodged in her throat, beating too hard and making it difficult to breathe easily. She tried to portray a sense of calm as Holden drove at rapid speed, back toward Evening and her farm.

Her farm. Her animals. Would they be okay? She couldn't even think of it. She had to put them out of her mind. She just…had to.

Holden had explained to her the brief exchange he'd had with Shay on the phone, and it worried her. Why would anyone go there? Even if they knew she had the evidence—which she herself hadn't yet decoded even if Holden's group had—they had to know after the fight this afternoon that she wasn't home.

"Maybe I could try to call Shay on your phone and give her some info. There are places to hide. Security codes. I could give them information."

Holden didn't spare her a glance. "Elsie was already in your bunker."

Willa blinked, somewhat taken aback. "How?"

"We have skills, Willa. She needed to hack into

your computer to see if she could find anything pertinent about your parents."

"She… Why would you guys *hack* into my computer? I'm cooperating with you." She didn't know how offended to be. It wasn't really the time for it, but…he hadn't told her they were hacking her computer, either, and that didn't feel right.

This Elsie person had been combing through her files. Her *parents'* files. "Did it ever occur to you *that's* how they got information about me and that evidence?"

"Elsie knows more about computers than most of the people in the *world*," Holden replied, his gaze never leaving the road as he raced against time. "She knows what she was doing. If she'd thought someone tracked what she was doing, what was being communicated, she would have either stopped it or let us know."

"I could have given you or her the passwords. I could have *given* you access, if you'd asked."

"You could have. She still would have hacked around or whatever it is computer people do to make sure you weren't only showing us part of the information."

"We're on the same team."

"We've got a dangerous criminal group. Two spies. Their daughter who can fight like the devil and has a whole underground bunker system. You tried to run and you kept some things from me along the way. Let's not play the game of trust and being on the same team."

It hurt, but it also reminded her of something more important than her childish hurt. "I have a way to get in where no one can see us."

"We don't know where their men are, Willa. We have to—"

"Trust me, Holden. I have a way." She ordered him to take a hard left, so he did. She directed him down gravel roads and dirt roads, then over the open field that would lead to the back of her property. To one of the escape hatches her parents had put in. "Here. Stop here," she said when they reached a swell of earth, covered in sod. She got out of the car, and Holden followed. His eyes were assessing, and his hands rested on either gun at his hip.

"I need a gun too," she said.

He hesitated, and that hurt. But she had to bury it in reality. In what they had to do. "You have to trust me. We have to be in this together."

He curled his hand around her neck. His grip was tight and fierce as he held her so they were almost nose to nose. "I let you fight off that guy at the lake all on your own. I didn't want to, but I knew you could and would take care of it. There isn't a bigger gesture of trust I've got than that."

She wanted to cry. She wanted to kiss him. But all she could do was take the gun he offered, then walk up the small swell of earth. She knelt on the ground, felt around until her fingers brushed metal. She pulled up the pole, then pushed, twisted and gave it a hard yank. It unlocked the door, hidden under the piles of sod. She lifted the hatch.

"This leads to the underground room we were in the other day. We can get to the house or the barn. Whichever you want."

"How… Willa, are you sure your parents don't use this as some kind of…home base?"

"Of course not," Willa replied, without thinking it through. They'd always said it was about her protection. And why would her parents take the trouble to go underground here and not tell her? She didn't use the underground area much at all herself, but still, wouldn't she know if they were under there? Wouldn't they…let her know?

With a sinking feeling in her chest, she realized they probably wouldn't. Especially if they were working.

She shook her head. "We'll figure that out later. Come on." She climbed into the hole. It was narrow here at the opening. "You might have trouble fitting, but you need to pull that door closed behind you."

She heard his grumbling from behind her. The tunnel was dark and tight. She'd never used this portion. She wouldn't call herself claustrophobic, but this particular tunnel being so narrow had always bothered her.

She breathed slowly, deeply, as the light gradually faded and they were in complete darkness.

"Does it lock?"

"We can lock it from the command center," Willa said, her voice strained.

"You okay?"

"Yeah. Can't say I like this one. Just keep moving forward. I'll be able to tell when we're closer to the more reasonable tunnels." She crawled forward, knowing there was no backing out. She was stuck. She couldn't get out.

Breathe in, one, two, three. Breathe out.

The walls weren't closing in. It wasn't possible. Feeling like they were was only irrational fear.

"Willa, honey, you're panting."

It was strange. *Honey.* She liked it. That was silly, but if she thought about silly things like endearments, she wouldn't feel like she was being swallowed whole by the earth.

If she lived through this, and she rather planned to, she'd call him... Dear? Too old-fashioned. Babe? No, that felt all wrong. Maybe she'd just call him honey back. She liked it, and if she...

If *they* made it out alive. He had to survive, too.

She swallowed as a new fear took over. "Where should we go? The bunker?" She had to focus on the reality of the situation, not the dark, cramped tunnel. Not life and death. Just getting from point A to point B.

"House. I think that's where Shay would be. You wouldn't hear gunshots from inside the bunker, would you?"

"No."

"Then house. Definitely."

She crawled what felt like endless minutes until at last the tunnel ended in a bigger "room" that connected all the tunnels together. The tunnels that led to the bunker and house and other places on the property were all deep enough to walk through without crawling.

Thank God. She got to her feet and led him to the path to the TV room door. It was still dark since she hadn't been able to be in the main room and switch on the lights via the generator. So she had to feel her way, which kept her pace slower than she knew Holden wanted.

Finally, she reached the end of the tunnel. "Here we are. How do you want to do it?"

"I'm going to go first, okay? You'll wait until I give you the signal to follow. I don't know what we're walking into yet."

She didn't say anything. Her throat was tight. She couldn't see anything in the dark, but she could feel him there. She didn't want to lose that.

"Willa?"

She cleared her throat and reached forward, unlocking the clasp that kept the door in place. She pulled it open slowly and quietly. There was a panel still covering the opening, but light streamed in through the cracks and she could make him out in the dim light.

"Honey, don't cry," Holden said reaching out and touching her wet cheek.

She hadn't realized she was. She was too numb with fear to know tears were leaking out. She wiped them away with her sleeves. "No, I'm okay. Really." She sniffled. "It'll be fine. You just slide the panel to the left, slip out and let me know when I can come out."

His eyebrows drew together, as if trying to figure

out her emotional outburst. But what was there to figure out? She was scared. A woman could be strong and scared at the same time. Heck, women usually *had* to be both.

She straightened her shoulders and nodded him toward the panel. "Go on."

"All right." He reached out for the panel, but she found herself incapable of holding all these emotions in. She couldn't fight like her parents, ignoring love when they had to. She couldn't. "I love you. So please don't die," she blurted.

The kiss was sudden, fierce, and she nearly fell over. If Holden hadn't been holding her so tightly, she might have. When he released her, she knew this was the only thing she could have hoped for in the moment.

A kiss that felt too much like a goodbye.

"Same goes, Willa. Same goes," he muttered, and then he was sliding the panel open.

SAME GOES. You are an utter, bumbling moron. Even as Holden searched the room, the *same goes* echoed in his head and threatened to split his focus.

But there could only be one focus.

The house was eerily silent, sometimes interrupted by a creak or groan that would make Holden still as he tried to figure out if it was old-house noise or people-moving-around noise.

When he was certain the room itself was safe, he motioned Willa out from the tunnel. They worked together in silence to close up the door and replace the wall paneling. Once that was done, he took her hand.

He didn't have to tell her to be quiet, to follow him carefully. She knew. She understood.

Holden didn't hear gunshots or breaking glass. He hoped to God that didn't mean he was too late.

Willa's grip tightened on his. It gave him center and focus, her gripping him so fiercely. He had to be strong for her.

He eased forward into the hall that would take him to the living room. He didn't have a clue as to where anyone would be, but he might be able to tell something from the living room, where you could see the kitchen, stairs and upper half of the upstairs.

As he poked his head into the room, he immediately saw Shay and Granger next to the big picture window. A couch had been moved out of the way, and shoved in front of the front door.

Shay was sitting in the floor, Granger crouched over her. Though the curtains were drawn, Holden saw the shattered glass littering the floor. Holden had to assume someone had shot through it.

It was a strange thing to see Granger McMillan standing there. He'd been the one to offer Holden a job in North Star, and like many of the other operatives, Holden had looked up to him like he'd been some kind of saint. Definitely a hero.

Then Granger had been shot in the explosion that had left scars on Holden's side. Granger's recovery had gone well enough, but he'd never returned to North Star.

Holden had to admit Granger didn't look the same.

He sported a heavy beard. Holden might have expected him to look wan, or rangy, but he'd done the opposite, adding a bulk that appeared to be all muscle, as if he'd spent his off time purposefully building himself into a different man.

"What happened?" Holden asked, keeping his voice low.

"Bit of an ambush. Not sure who's out there, or how many, but suddenly they were shooting up the house. We held them off, but…" Shay trailed off, staring at them more closely. "How did you guys get in here?"

"Tunnels under the house, came in through the inside. Are they still out there?"

"I think so. We don't have enough to recon. I've got a backup team coming, but I told them to proceed with extreme caution since we've got nothing on what's going on out there."

Holden frowned at the way Shay was still sitting and had one hand clamped over her arm.

"What's wrong with you?" he demanded.

"Nothing. I'm fine."

"She's not."

"I *am*."

"She got shot."

"I got *clipped*. In the arm. Hell, for all we know it was a piece of glass. I'm fine."

"She won't let me field dress it."

Holden muttered an oath. "Don't be stupid. Get it dressed. Where's Elsie?"

"In that godforsaken bunker," Shay ground out, glaring daggers at Granger. "I want her to stay there."

"She's seeing what she can do to hack into the security measures, but it takes time," Granger offered, but his attention was on grappling with Shay to get her arm free so he could dress it. "She says it's quite the encrypted system. She can kick through it, but there's hoops to jump through and whatnot."

"I'll go. I'll go help," Willa said, her hand still in his. "I can get video and security measures all up in five minutes tops. It doesn't seal off the whole farm, but it'll make things more difficult for anyone trying to get within the property lines."

"Not sure security measures are going to help when they're already here," Holden said, though he knew that was emotion more than sense talking. Still, he had to say it. He had to…

Willa grabbed his arm, eyes wide and determined. "Let me go do this. I know the tunnels, how to get in and out fast and easy. You three hold the fort here. You just get a message to Elsie so she knows to look for me. It'll help. You know it will."

"We shouldn't separate," Holden said, but Willa was already moving away as if he'd agreed.

He swore under his breath. "Fine. Go. But get everything set up, then I want you and Elsie up here." They all needed to be together where he could be certain they were protected.

"Okay. I will." She dropped his hand and arm and scurried off, and Holden had to fight down all his instincts to stay where he was and not chase after her.

"Do me a favor and knock Shay out so I can get this wrapped around the wound," Granger grumbled.

He'd torn a piece of fabric from his own shirt, and if Willa wasn't off in those tunnels alone, Holden might have found some humor in the situation. "Best not to knock her out. We might need all hands on deck." He glanced at Shay. "Why are you being so difficult?"

"Because this moron disobeyed a direct order."

"I'm your superior," Granger muttered, taking the arm she reluctantly held out.

The gash was deep, but Holden had to admit it looked more like a cut from glass than a bullet. She'd need stitches, but it'd hold for now.

"No, you left," Shay said through gritted teeth as Granger inspected the wound, then wrapped the strip of fabric around it. "*And* left me in charge. You're of ficially a subordinate."

"I didn't even want to get roped back into this—"

A gunshot rang out from outside, but wherever it hit the house wasn't close to them. It seemed to knock Granger and Shay out of their argument.

They all were on their feet, guns out and ready, in seconds flat.

"Shay, get that message to Elsie so she knows not to shoot Willa. Then go to the bunker. There's something about this place that gives me a bad feeling. Granger, take east. I'll take west."

"You're not in charg—"

But he had no reason to listen to Shay's orders when they didn't know who or what they were up against. Besides, Shay might be his boss, but this was *his* mission. He'd come to believe that bunker and the tunnels were more than just safeguarding Willa.

What? He didn't know. But he wanted Willa in and out ASAP.

Another gunshot exploded somewhere in the dark night. As far as Holden could tell by listening, that one hadn't hit the house.

Which raised the question…if someone out there wasn't shooting at the house, what were they shooting at?

Chapter Nineteen

Willa had never been afraid of the dark that she could remember. When she'd been very young, her parents had trained her how to move in the dark. How to keep her calm in the dark. How to defend herself in the dark.

Willa felt as if all those lessons had deserted her. She had to force herself into the dark tunnels again. Though she gratefully didn't have to crawl through the narrow one, something about this oppressive dark made her feel like everything was all wrong.

But she had to get to the bunker. Video would help Holden's team figure out what they were up against. The security measures she could enact didn't have the potential to eradicate the threat, but they could definitely diminish it.

Holden needed her help. She blew out a breath as she felt through the tunnel, ducking as it got a little shorter as went from under the house to outside. It would get taller again when she was under the barn and nearing the bunker.

She hadn't had a chance to ask after her animals.

There was too much danger to worry how the crew was holding up. She could only offer up a silent prayer that in the light of morning every person and every animal would be safe.

Please God.

She stepped forward, the ceiling a more walkable height yet again. She let out a soft whoosh of breath. There were a few hurdles left. First, Elsie had to have gotten the message that the woman who would walk into the bunker wasn't an enemy. Second, if Elsie had engaged any of the locks from the inside, she would have to *hear* Willa pounding or yelling at the door, and then want to open it.

Yelling would be a bad idea. As much as she doubted her voice would carry through subterranean tunnels, she didn't want to risk anything.

Are you sure your parents don't use this as some kind of...home base?

She didn't know why that question of Holden's bothered her, why it kept popping up in her head. So what if they did? It would be their right. Yes, her feelings might be hurt if they were underfoot and never told her, but they'd built the tunnels.

To keep you safe.

If they hadn't done it for that reason, it hardly mattered. Either way, they weren't the bad guys here, so even if they used them, it didn't matter.

Willa stumbled to a stop as a dim light spread out into the tunnel. It was the door opening. A tall figure stepping out into the swath of light.

Willa's breath caught, then she raced forward, tears

springing to her eyes. "Dad. Dad. Oh my God." She practically fell into his arms. She furiously blinked back the tears, holding on to him tight. He was alive. He was okay. He was here. "Oh, thank God you're okay." A panicky laugh escaped her mouth. "Here. Oh, thank God."

"Wills." He sounded almost surprised, but his arms were strong and tight around her.

"Where's Mom? She's okay, isn't she?" She had to be. Had to be. Willa pulled back to look at her father's face.

"She's not far away," Dad said, an odd, sad smile on his face. He brought up his hands to her cheeks, searching her face. He sighed. "What happened to you?"

Willa reached up and touched the bandage on her head. "It's been a strange few days." She was tempted to tell him *everything*, but now was not the time. "Where have you been?"

Dad glanced at the room behind them. Willa couldn't see Mom or Elsie, but surely they were in there. "It's a very long story." He sighed, then looked back at her. "But you're here. Which is good. Everything will be okay now that you're here." He smoothed down her hair, and Willa gave in to the luxury of hugging her father as tight as she could.

He expelled a breath that was something like a mix of pain and relief. "I am so, so sorry, Willa," he said into her ear.

"Sorry?" She wanted to laugh again, but she pulled away from him instead. "But you're here."

There was something about his eyes, about the odd slant of his mouth that had her backing up.

He frowned a little. "What are you doing? Mom's just inside." He swept a hand toward the entrance, and Willa found herself taking full steps back. Away from her father. A man she'd always loved unconditionally, without suspicion.

But something was wrong. Something was *all* wrong.

"Come in," he insisted. "We have a lot to talk about."

But a cold dread settled through her. She didn't want to go in.

She was being ridiculous. Of course she needed to go inside. Her parents would take care of everything, like they always did.

Except the past few days.

The past few days. Nothing had made sense. This certainly didn't. She was being…foolish to question it.

Except her parents had always told her to listen to dread. No emotional outbursts, but by God, a spy had to listen to their gut. She didn't want to go in there. She didn't want to understand why her father's expression was so…off. Sad. Resigned. And just a little lost.

None of those things had ever been her father.

"Dad. Tell me what's going on."

"On?"

Her dread intensified. "There are men shooting at my house. You've been ignoring my SOS messages, or, as I thought, had been taken or killed by someone so *couldn't* respond. But here you are, apologizing and then acting like something isn't going on?"

"Come inside, Wills. Your mother was always better at explaining things than I was."

"Then call her out here."

"Willa." He sounded hurt. She believed him for a second, but none of it made sense. *None* of it.

And then there was a gun. In her father's hand. Lifting toward her. No, it didn't make sense, and no, she didn't want to believe this of her father, but when a gun was pointed at a person, there were only a few options.

She chose to run. Back into the dark. Back to Holden. It was all wrong. *All* wrong, but Holden wasn't. He'd save her.

No, Willa, it's time to save yourself.

She zigzagged as much as she could in the narrow tunnel. The gun didn't go off, and she had to be grateful he wasn't shooting blindly in the dark.

Maybe he hadn't meant to shoot at her at all. Maybe she was being paranoid and reading everything wrong.

Well, that was something she'd figure out, but she wasn't about to risk it. Even when it came to her own father.

She was running too hard, breathing too heavily to hear anything. Was he chasing her? Had he given up?

Is any of this real?

Someone slammed into her hard, and she fell to the ground. If it was her father and he had the gun still, he didn't use it. They wrestled on the cold, hard ground. Willa fought tooth and nail, but her opponent was stronger, better in the dark.

"We have to end it." Dad's voice, breathless and strained. He worked to get a hold of her arms and pin them down, so she fought wildly. Punching, kicking, wriggling away.

"They can torture me, I don't care," he continued. "But I won't give them you. I won't let them do that to you."

Willa didn't understand what was happening, what he meant, but she knew she couldn't give in to it. "Then let me go," she said, trying to push him off her.

"You'll never be free. We'll never be free. It has to end."

Willa didn't want to know what he meant by that, but she had the sinking suspicion she knew exactly what he wanted.

He wanted to die, and her to go with him.

THERE WAS THE occasional sound of gunfire, but nothing close. The lack of lights outside kept them from seeing who or what might be out there. The lack of full-frontal attack made Holden's nerves hum.

Three of the windows on the main level had been shattered by gunfire. Holden considered heading upstairs. It might give him a better vantage point, but the incessant dark of the country night wouldn't allow him to see anything.

Besides, he didn't want to be that far away from the tunnels and Willa.

Whoever was out there wasn't out there to attack.

Or, if they were, they were supposed to wait, hold back, break a few windows. It was attention seeking at best.

Holden met up with Granger after their inside perimeter check. "Any word from Shay?" Holden asked.

"No."

"Should have heard something by now," Holden said with a frown. "This isn't anything. What's with the random gunfire? Surely they don't think there's an army in here. They're waiting for something."

"Elsie was getting somewhere with that computer, but she hadn't briefed us yet when the guns started. Do you think they could tell she'd gotten the information they want?"

"How?" That was the question that plagued Holden. *How?* "None of this adds up, Granger, and you know as well as I do that means we don't know what they're really after."

"So, we'll figure it out."

"They're just there to hold our attention, or maybe make sure we don't run. They're not attacking."

"They could be amassing more men or ammunition or something. They could be working to blow us up."

Could, Holden thought. But it didn't feel right. He thought of Willa in the tunnels, and Shay. They weren't back yet, and there was no attempt at contact. "Unless someone else is down there."

"You think that's possible?" Granger returned, his eyes staring out the gap between curtain and window where they stood in the TV room. "Elsie acted like there was no way in or out."

"If you didn't know where to look," Holden muttered. "Let's go down there."

"And leave the house unprotected?"

"Screw the house," Holden replied, already moving to the other room. Shay had left the panel off, and he couldn't blame her for that. The door was closed though.

Or was. It swung open as Holden reached for it, Shay stumbling quickly into the light. She squinted against it, panting.

"Someone's fighting down there. I need a light. We need someone at the other entrance. I don't know if they got in or what, but we've got to move."

The only people who could be fighting in the tunnel were Willa and someone else, unless two new people had entered the tunnel from who knew were.

"You two to the barn and the other opening. I'll take the light to the tunnel."

"Holden." Shay didn't say more, and Holden refused to parse what the expression on her face meant. He had a flashlight on him, and he was going to get to Willa.

He nudged Shay out of the way and moved into the tunnel. He pulled the door closed behind him, plunging the world around him into darkness.

He took one deep breath to get his eyes as accustomed to the dark as he was going to get, then he moved forward. He held his gun in one hand, flashlight in the other. He kept it off. Though Shay had claimed someone was fighting, Holden heard nothing.

Moving forward carefully and stealthily was a battle in restraint he was slowly losing. He wanted to run and race forward. He wanted to bellow Willa's name. But none of those things would get her out of this alive.

She had to be the one who'd been fighting. There was no other explanation. Maybe she'd won and gotten to Elsie in the bunker. She could do it. He had faith in her.

But still he moved forward, dread solid and heavy in his gut. When things didn't add up, what a man believed and had faith in didn't always add up either.

After what felt like eons, Holden saw what he thought might be…light. He moved forward until it became clear there was indeed the tiniest sliver of light. It was the door to the bunker, just barely ajar.

Holden moved toward it. Quietly, he moved until he was as close to the door as he could get without pushing it open.

He heard a voice, and it made his blood run cold. Because that was a man's voice, and as far as he knew, only women were down here.

Chapter Twenty

Willa didn't know if she'd fully lost consciousness, but a blow to her already wounded temple had made her woozy enough to forget to fight. It made her forget what she was fighting for. She could feel her body, and she could *feel* herself being dragged into the bunker. She even watched as Dad tied her up.

Willa stared, uncomprehending, at the nylon rope pulled tight around her arms. She could move her legs, but she didn't know what to do with them. The ground was cold under her, but there was something warm and soft next to her. A light scent, faint, like a memory.

"Willa, baby."

Was that her mother's voice? Willa told herself to look toward it, but she couldn't seem to turn her head. She couldn't seem to make her body do any of the things it should.

Was she already dead? But she heard her mother's voice, and something that sounded like a sob. No, that wasn't right. Her mother didn't cry. She had to be dreaming.

You need to wake up, then.

But there was pain and confusion, and she kept shying away from taking a grip on full consciousness. This fog seemed better. Safer. She could make things make sense here. Nothing made sense outside the fog.

"Willa. Talk to me, sweetheart." Mom's voice was more like a whisper now. Was it really her mother? Maybe she was hallucinating. But there was a warm body next to her.

Willa had no idea how long it took her to find the strength to turn her head, toward the voice, toward the warmth. She tried to blink and focus as a face wavered in her vision. Close. So close.

Mom's green eyes. The nose so like Willa's own. Her mother. Not a figment of her imagination. Not some after-life hallucination, because Willa could see her. Feel her pressed next to her.

"Mom," she managed to croak.

"It's going to be okay," Mom said fiercely. But there were tears in Mom's eyes, and Willa didn't know how things could be okay if her mother was crying. Her mother was a spy. A woman trained to withstand torture, to take down any threat in her way.

But big, fat tears rolled down Mom's cheeks.

Everything was so woozy, so off. Willa knew she had to find some strength, some concentration. Her head pounded, but something had to be done. Mom was crying. That wasn't right. Willa had to find the strength to make something right.

"This wasn't how it was supposed to go," Dad was muttering, pacing in front of them.

Dad. Who'd fought her, hurt her and then dragged her inside the bunker. The bunker. Willa squinted through the pain and the fog and tried to understand her surroundings.

She was sitting on the ground, shoulder to shoulder with Mom, who was shoulder to shoulder with another woman. That woman had to be Elsie. She was completely still, her head nodded forward. Willa would have thought she was dead, but she wasn't particularly pale, and there was a slight rise and fall of her chest.

"Alive, but drugged," Mom whispered, her gaze following Dad going back and forth in front of them.

He slapped the barrel of the gun against his palm as he moved. His eyes looked even wilder in the full light of the bunker. Willa could clearly see the fear in her own mother's eyes.

The gray fog threatened to take over again. Safer there. Easier there. But the cold trickle of fear cut through her ability to fully let go.

"It has to end. It has to end. We have to end it," Dad said. Over and over and over.

Willa knew she wasn't functioning at full capacity, but she still understood her father wasn't…sane. Panic crept through the gray cloud of pain and centered her in the here and now. Her temple throbbed violently. Both an outside burning feeling where she was sure she was bleeding, and an inside bone-deep pointed pain.

And still Dad paced. Willa didn't think he'd always

been like this. God, she hoped the man she'd known and loved hadn't been an act with this underneath.

But whoever was pacing in front of them now was not the father she loved. Who'd taught her how to fight, who'd protected her. This was someone else.

He'd tied her up. He'd tied *Mom* up. And poor Elsie, who had nothing to do with her family's current problems except she was part of a group trying to stop a hit man.

How did it all connect? Holden and Shay and Mom and Dad and the men who'd shot at her house?

"I don't understand anything that is going on," Willa said, thought it felt a bit like someone else had said it. Like she was two different people—the body and the brain, severed.

Except she'd said the words and Mom was weeping quietly next to her.

"There's nothing to understand, Wills. Nothing," Dad said firmly. "Too many mistakes. The mistakes have to be corrected. I have to correct them."

Mom took a deep breath beside her, and when she spoke, whatever trace of upset and tears were gone. She was calm and forceful. "William, look at me."

But Dad only shook his head. "Have to be corrected," he mumbled, still tapping the gun. "They want us dead. There's no escape."

"We have always escaped before," Mom said, but her voice cracked at the last word. "William. Please."

Dad's head shaking grew more violent. "No, no, no. Too late. It's over. It has to be over. I have to end it." He stopped moving abruptly, looking straight at Willa. "She has to be first."

Willa tried not to react. Or cry. She tried to hold on to the gray fog, but it kept lifting, leaving her with more and more clarity that the chances of her making out of this alive were getting slimmer and slimmer.

"William! She is your daughter." Mom's voice was like an odd echo, followed by sobs that couldn't be coming from her mother. Her mother was too strong. Too brave.

"We should have done this a long time ago. All three of us. Until we're all dead, they can hurt us. But once we're dead, they can't."

He was going to kill her. Willa couldn't reconcile it. Even as the gun was pointed at her, and she knew her father would pull the trigger. Purposefully. With the intent to end her life.

Mom was screaming and sobbing now, fighting the bonds around them, trying to maneuver her body in front of Willa's. But Willa knew it wouldn't matter.

He wanted them both dead. To end it.

He held the gun steady. His eyes were cold, detached. "They can torture me, but I won't let them torture you. We've been found out. Our cover is blown. We're surrounded. There's no escape this time. They can get what they need out of me. But not you. I won't let them hurt my girls."

Dad's voice broke. Mom was sobbing. Willa couldn't find it within her to cry or plead. She didn't know how to argue with his words when she hardly knew who was after them. What they were up against or what had caused him to break with reality.

Besides, he was too far gone. His mind had broken, cracked into something deranged.

All Willa could do was close her eyes and hope for some kind of miracle.

THE WEEPING GREW louder as Holden inched forward. He could hear the voices but still couldn't see anyone in the main room yet.

He forced himself to focus on the entryway to the main room. The brighter light. The angles. He couldn't think about the weeping. Whether it was Willa. If she was hurt. That would split his focus. It might make his hand shake when he had to be nothing but cold. Precise.

He had to do everything in his power to get Willa out of there unharmed.

He got close to the main room entrance then paused, straining to hear over the quiet crying.

"No, no, no. Too late," a man's voice was saying. "It's over. It has to be over. I have to end it. She has to be first."

A woman's voice rang out. It started tough and authoritative but gradually got desperately panicked. "William! She is your daughter."

She. The she had to be Willa. These were Willa's parents? That would explain how they'd known to get into the tunnels, but why would the dad be talking about ending it? What did Willa have to be first to do?

He thought about just walking in. If Willa was with

her parents, surely they'd taken care of whoever she was fighting with. Surely things were okay.

But something—a gut feeling, a deeper understanding he didn't fully comprehend yet—kept him where he was. Listening. Waiting.

"We should have done this a long time ago," the man said. "All three of us. Until we're all dead, they can hurt us. But once we're dead, they can't."

Immediately Holden moved closer, until he could actually see into most of the room. Willa, the woman he assumed was her mother and a slumped-over Elsie were tied together in a corner. A tall, slender man holding a gun paced in front of them.

Holden raised his own weapon. He could take the shot to kill. In another situation, he wouldn't have thought twice. But this was Willa's father. He couldn't…do that in front of her. Not while she was watching.

But he could hardly let her die, and if the man was dead set on killing his own wife and daughter, a shot aimed only to injure might end up with him still getting off a shot on Willa or her mother or Elsie.

He could make a noise, try to lure Willa's father out toward him, but that could also force the man's hand and make him shoot quicker. Right now, with a pacing man, muttering nonsense, there was still a chance he didn't talk himself into shooting them.

As long as Holden didn't force his hand.

There was no good solution. Nothing he could do that didn't risk Willa. Holden held his gun steady, trained on the pacing man. As long as he wasn't acting, as long as the gun was tapping against his palm and not pointed at anyone, Holden had a chance to come up with a solution.

He racked his mind for any possible end result, but he was distracted by a tapping sound behind him. Soft, but distinct. A North Star code. He looked over his shoulder and saw Shay and Granger coming through the tunnel exit.

Holden held up a hand, a nonverbal silence sign. There was no time to express his relief, no way to ask them why they'd come this way and not through the outdoor bunker entrance, and he couldn't risk being heard to explain everything he needed to explain to them.

He had to rely on rudimentary battlefield hand signals and hope to God they understood. Both nodded as if they did, so Holden motioned them close.

They huddled together in the opening between back room and main room. Holden gave himself a moment to breathe, to center. To focus on the end result.

Willa and Elsie safe. Nothing else really mattered.

"On go," Holden said under his breath, knowing his voice would be muffled by the sound of crying coming from inside the room. "No loss of life," he added, because the last thing he wanted for Willa, even knowing her father was the bad guy in this situation, was for her to have to *watch* him die.

Holden would do whatever he could to spare her that. If it meant risking his own life. He wouldn't leave her with that image. What she was enduring now was bad enough.

He wouldn't let her die, and he wouldn't hurt her more than she'd already been hurt.

He breathed, watched, listened. The man began to speak again.

"They can torture me, but I won't let them torture you. We've been found out. Our cover is blown. We're surrounded. There's no escape this time. They can get what they need out of me. But not you. I won't let them hurt my girls."

He began to raise the gun to point at Willa. Directly at Willa.

"Go!"

As Holden had hoped, the sudden yell drew Willa's father's attention to him and not Willa. Holden, Shay and Granger moved into the bunker as one.

Willa's father swung the gun toward them, but his angle would hit Shay, so Holden shot at the man's arm. There was a howl of pain, and the gun he'd been holding clattered to the floor. He didn't fall to the ground, and another gunshot rang out.

Granger shooting to get the man off his feet.

Holden didn't have time to regret it as blood bloomed on Willa's father's shirt and he grabbed his side and stumbled backward.

Shay was already untying the three women, and the one Holden assumed was Willa's mother immediately scrambled forward to her husband. Granger was wrestling the man's arms into a submissive position, and Willa's mother wasn't impeding his progress at all. She was just crying and murmuring things to her thrashing husband. Granger had it under control, so Holden turned to Willa and Elsie.

Elsie was completely limp. Shay moved to her immediately, checking vital signs when Elsie didn't move even once the ropes were off.

"Mom said she was drugged. I don't know what or how, but she's not dead. She's breathing," Willa was saying, pushing the now-lax rope off her.

She didn't immediately stand up. Her wound from yesterday was bleeding again, and she was pale as death. "Did he hurt you?" Holden demanded.

"He…" She looked at where her father lay on the ground. Then back up at Holden, green eyes heartbreakingly vulnerable. "Is he going to die?"

"I…don't know." He didn't know how to lie to her, but the expression that crossed her face —pain and a sense of loss that he had to assume was more than one kind of loss—made him wish he had.

He held out a hand and helped her to her feet. She wavered once upright, and Holden grabbed her before she fell over. Then he simply…held on. Somehow he was murmuring things, and he wasn't even sure what. Just that she was okay and it would somehow be okay. It was a jumble even to his own ears.

Willa sobbed quietly into his shoulders, her fingers digging into his back as he held on. Vaguely he heard Shay on the phone with Betty asking for any kind of medical backup they could get, but to be careful.

Careful, because there were still men out there.

"They said they were surrounded. What does that mean?"

Willa sniffled and shook her head. Though she pulled her head off her shoulder, she didn't release him and he didn't release her. "I don't know. I don't understand anything that's going on. Mom…"

Willa's mother turned from her husband. He was lying still, but Granger was still holding pressure on the stomach wound. Shay was on the phone, cradling Elsie's head in her lap, giving instructions to Granger, likely relayed from Betty, on how to stop the bleeding.

It was a madhouse, and they still weren't safe.

"We were undercover, working for Ross Industries. Our assignment was to get the names of two possible hit men targets. We'd gotten them, but we were made before we could relay the information. William and I ran for it, coming here. We thought the bunker, but…" She looked back at her husband. "He…snapped. He told them where we were. He said we had to end it."

When she looked up at Holden, he saw Willa's green eyes, heartbreaking and devastated. "This isn't him. I don't know what happened. He just…cracked."

Holden looked at Shay and Granger. They were still hovering over the man like he had a chance to live.

But they had to get out of here first.

Chapter Twenty-One

He just cracked.

Willa felt an odd relief. Her father wasn't evil. He'd been good. He'd been the man she'd thought. He'd just *cracked.* But that knowledge did nothing to help the situation.

She couldn't seem to stop clinging to Holden, but they were still in danger, and they had to get Dad to some kind of medical center. They *had* to.

"What about the hit man who got ammunition here?" Holden asked Mom.

Mom looked down at Dad once more, then slowly got to her feet. She took a deep breath and straightened her shoulders. "He was picking up the ammunition and one of the names. I met with him myself."

"And gave him the name?" Holden asked incredulously.

She shrugged. "It was the job, and the only way to get the name and get out in one piece. William and I were supposed to be out by now, reporting the name to our superiors."

"You haven't yet?" Willa asked breathlessly. She

looked wildly around at Shay and the man who'd come in with her, then Holden. Panic rose. Someone was out there going about their life about to be killed? Willa couldn't stomach it. She couldn't *stand* it. "We have to. We have to get the names to whoever will stop them. No one should die."

"People die in this world, Willa," Mom said, looking down at Dad's still body.

Willa looked up at Holden, desperate to find someone who agreed. Who understood. But his mouth was grim, and his eyes were unreadable.

And still he held her.

"We need to think this through strategically. We have injured people who need medical attention. How many men are surrounding the house?"

Mom moved around Dad's too-still form and went for the computer. "I can bring up the generators and the computer. That'll get video on them. Willa?"

Willa knew Mom was asking her to help. Together they could get all the systems up and going faster. But she was loath to stop holding on to Holden. He felt like an anchor. Like a safe port in storm.

But her father was likely dying, after suffering a psychotic break, and she didn't want that to happen to anyone else here.

She released Holden and stepped over to her mother. "Why can't we go out the south field exit?"

Mom looked back at Dad. "He destroyed it."

Willa swallowed against the panic and moved to get the generator running.

"What about the names?" Holden asked. Everything about him flat and unreadable, but he was asking about the names. Willa found something unwind inside her.

They could do this. Good could fight and win.

"I can tell you one, but not the other. Only William knows the other."

Everyone in the room looked down at Dad. Pale. Blood dripping onto the floor no matter how much Granger held pressure on it.

"We thought it'd be safer that way. If one of us got caught…" Mom trailed off. She shook her head and focused on the computer. "That's why we left Willa some evidence, too. Coded. We just wanted her to have some leverage. But William…told them." Mom swallowed. "When they found us out, he told them everything. That's why they wanted to kidnap her."

Willa closed her eyes against a wave of pain and fear and then turned to focus her attentions on the generator. She couldn't look at Dad. She'd break right along with him. She had to focus on the generator. On the danger.

She didn't know anything about the hit man's targets. Maybe they weren't that good of people anyway. Still, fear and guilt ate away at her insides like acid. It wasn't fair whoever the targets were might die simply because they were stuck here or that Dad might die.

Might die.

Just cracked.

After a few long, excruciating minutes Mom got the cameras up and began studying the images. Though the tracks of tears were evident on her face, and her eyes were red and puffy, she appeared calm and in control. An expert spy.

He just cracked.

Shay hung up the phone. "We've got ten on the ground. It's the most we can get before morning."

"How many men do you think your ten can take out?" Mom asked, her eyes sharp on the computer as she tapped at keys, bringing up the infrared censors that would be able to pick up video in the dark—a feature Willa hadn't even been aware of.

Willa thought of what Holden said about Mom and Dad using this when she didn't know it, and it had to be true. It had to be true. Willa shook it away. Didn't matter now. All that mattered was survival.

Mom studied the different video screens. She was pale and clearly shaken, but Willa could see in this moment she was a spy. She was doing her duty, no matter what mistakes Dad had made.

"Twenty to thirty, depending."

"It doesn't look like we've got more than fifteen. I don't know their backup situation, but I wouldn't think it'd be on-site since they should think there's only two of us here." She glanced at Holden, then Elsie on the ground. "I don't know if they knew about you."

Shay nodded. "We'll take the chance. We've got a medic team waiting to transport to the closest hospital."

"Both of them, or just yours?" Mom asked. There was no bitterness in her voice. Just a weary kind of acceptance.

"Both," Holden answered firmly, brooking no argument from Shay or Granger.

"I'll give my team the signal to move," Shay said, sitting with Elsie's head in her lap, and somehow looking every bit the fierce leader of her group. "I've got contact with my lead, and he'll relay orders to his team."

"Wait to have them move," Holden said. "Give me five. I'm going to go out."

"No," Willa felt herself say without fully thinking it through.

"It'll make it eleven men on the ground," Holden said firmly, but he wasn't looking at her. He was looking at Shay. "You two stay here with Elsie and…him. Betty told you how to take care of them in the meantime. Here, I'm superfluous. I might as well be out there helping the team."

This time Willa said her no with more force, with more intent. "You can't just go out there."

"Yes, I can."

Shay tossed him something, and he caught it easily, immediately hooking it to his ear. Some kind of earpiece. "He'll keep in touch," Shay said, and Willa knew it was for her benefit. "It connects to my phone. You and your mom can relay what you see to him and the rest of the team."

Shay carefully moved Elsie's head off her lap, gently laying it on the floor. She stood and began to pull off the heavy black vest she was wearing.

"I'm not taking your vest," Holden said irritably. "You might need it here."

"That's only if they get through you first, which, if you have a vest, there's less chance of. Take it."

"Please," Willa added. "Please take it."

Holden scowled, but he walked over to Shay and took the vest. He loosened the straps then fitted it over his head. "There? Happy?"

She wasn't. Even a little. She moved from the generator to him. Too many fears. Too many possible outcomes. So much bad had already happened. She wasn't sure how much strength she had left. So she didn't reach out and touch him. She just looked at him and felt like her insides were being crushed by bricks. She could feel tears welling in her eyes, but she used all her strength not to shed them. "Just…be careful."

Holden leaned down and gave her a quick, hard kiss. "Don't leave this bunker until it's safe."

Then he was gone. In a blink. Willa stared after him. Gone into the dark. Where men with guns were waiting.

"Who is he?" Mom murmured.

Willa didn't know what to say or how to explain. All she had was one simple truth. "I love him."

"Well, I can tell *that*, but who *is* he?"

Willa turned back to Mom and the computers and the work they had to do to keep Holden and the rest of his group safe. "A very good man."

HOLDEN MOVED THROUGH the night. It was familiar, routine, habit. It was an assignment like any other. Except the odd, terrifying need to get back in one piece.

He'd never had anyone to get back *to*. At least not

since he'd started down this path. North Star might have become his family, but he'd never fully thought of what they might feel if he was hurt or dead. So he'd never had this ever-present nagging worry that he had to avoid it.

The earpiece crackled. "Headed straight for a group of three. Reroute east a good bit and you might be able to sneak around behind them and meet some of your own men." It wasn't Shay's voice in his ear—it was a woman he didn't recognize. Which meant it had to be Willa's mother.

That felt a little weird, but he followed her instructions. As far as he could tell, she was on the up and up, unlike her husband.

He moved east, circled around back. He tapped a tree softly, using the North Star code to announce his presence. He listened for the reply, and once he heard it approached.

It was Gabe and an operative named Mallory. Gabe gestured toward the group of three they were watching, then laid out the plan of action in field signals.

Approach and, if undetected, subdue. If detected, shoot to debilitate.

Holden nodded, and then they moved through the dark and the trees.

The voice in his ear got loud. "You've got two on your back. Now."

Holden whirled as the first shot went off. He wasn't sure if it hit anyone, but he immediately shot back. One stumbled but didn't lose his footing. "Gabe and Mal, stay up front. I'll take these two."

They spoke their assent, more gunfire echoing through the night. It was hard to aim in the dark, though sound and the woman's voice in his ear helped.

"Ten o'clock and three o'clock," she said, giving him enough of an idea about where his attackers were to shoot in the general direction. He was pretty sure he got one, but an explosion hit his chest before he could fire another shot.

The bullet hitting his vest was hard enough to knock the breath out of him, and he stumbled backward and fell on his butt. He didn't lose his gun, but he landed awkwardly enough it was going to take precious seconds to get back into shooting position.

Precious seconds he didn't have. Holden was prepared to roll onto the ground and hope for the best when he heard the sounds of pounding...not feet. Too light to be feet. Then there was a growl, the sounds of snapping teeth. Followed by the high-pitched scream of someone Holden didn't think was on his team.

"Get it off me! Get it off me!" the voice he didn't recognize yelled.

A flashlight beam clicked on. Gabe's. He swung it around, counting out the three bodies they'd taken out on one side. On the other side, one body was crumpled on the ground. The other was writhing and screaming as a dog bit his arm. His gun arm.

"Jim."

The dog stopped, then trotted over to Holden as if nothing had happened. Mallory swept in, collecting all the guns. Gabe tied up the man who was still screaming about the wolf attack.

"It was a dog, dude," Gabe said. "Perfectly nice one," he added, gesturing to where Holden still sat on his butt.

Holden reached out and scratched Jim behind the ears. "You might have saved my life, bud."

The dog plopped down next to Holden and contentedly let Holden pet him while Holden listened to the instructions in his earpiece.

"You've got all of them. Shay's sending in the medic team. Your orders are to follow, flanking them in case of more men."

"Got it," Holden muttered, loosening the straps on the damn vest. His chest hurt like hell and he couldn't quite get a full breath, but he was alive. Thank God for that.

Holden got up, Jim getting to his feet and following close by Holden wherever he walked. Gabriel relayed the orders to the rest of the team, and they waited for the medic team to emerge, then fanned out in a careful protective line. Jim never left Holden's side.

In the end, that was it. They waited and waited as the medical team entered the bunker, as they got Willa's father and Elsie out and into the transport vehicle. No one came. Aside from the FBI anyway.

Inside Willa's house was a hub of activity. Different groups appraising other groups, getting facts and information straight. Holden had to sit with one FBI agent for far too long, and when he was done, there was one person Holden didn't see in the crowd.

He tapped Shay's arm, drawing her away from the heated argument she was having with Granger.

"Where's Willa?"

Shay looked around, frowning. "I'm not sure. Maybe you should ask her mom? Vera's over there talking to some suit from the FBI."

But Holden didn't want to interrupt or worry Willa's mother when he didn't have to. When he looked down at Jim still next to him, Holden suddenly knew exactly where she'd be.

He walked back outside, Jim following, and to the barn. The sun was beginning to rise, but the world was mostly still dark. There was a dim light shining from inside. He stepped in to find her exactly where he'd thought, and yet so much more *her* than he'd realized.

Not just with her animals, but sitting on the floor of the barn surrounded by them. A cat on her lap, goats behind her. Dogs everywhere.

His chest hurt more, but it wasn't the nasty bruise he'd likely have from the impact of the bullet on the vest. It was just her.

He didn't know what to say. There were too many *feelings*. Because her part in this was over and she was safe and now…

What now?

"Hi," she offered. "Everyone's here and okay, but I can't seem to find…" She trailed off as Jim trotted in behind him.

"Pretty sure your dog saved my life," Holden managed. She looked so fragile there, sitting in hay surrounded by animals. Someone had rebandaged her head, and the gauze was a stark white against her ashen face and reddish hair.

Jim trotted over to Willa, and she simply buried her face in the dog's fur and gave him a tight squeeze. "Aren't you brave and clever," she murmured to the dog.

"I like to think so," Holden replied, hoping to make her smile.

She looked up at him. Her lips almost curved, but it was hardly a smile. She just stared at him for the longest time.

Uncomfortable with the silence, Holden fidgeted. "Did your mom catch you up?"

She shook her head, still holding on to the dog for dear life. "No, she was still talking to…whoever and filling them in."

"Do you want to know?"

She looked down at the cat in her lap. She didn't answer. But he figured knowing might help her break through the shock she was surely feeling.

"Your father's in surgery. It'll be a while before we know how he'll fare, but he's still fighting."

She let out a breath. "Even if he lives, he'll go to jail."

"I think he'll get some psychiatric help first."

She sat with that for a minute, then finally looked up and met his gaze. "Elsie?"

"She's fine. They want her to stay overnight for observation, but she's recovering nicely. All the men we stopped have been arrested, and the Ross Industries warehouse is being raided by the feds."

Willa stroked the cat with one hand, the dog with

the other. A goat stood behind her quietly munching on something. Another cat sat on a pail in the corner, and three dogs lay as one in some hay right next to her. This was where she was meant to be. Not off chasing bad guys. Here. Living a real life. A normal life. Well, sort of normal.

Why did he suddenly want one of those?

"There's more, isn't there?" she asked on a sigh.

Holden didn't see how he could keep it from her. "There are still two hit men out there. Sabrina's already made progress on the name your mother gave us, and she had information about the second name. So we're doing everything we can to save both men."

"Why would the hit men still kill them if there's no one to pay them?"

"We don't think Ross Industries is the only group involved. Just another arm. But we cut off this one. That's something."

"Ah." She nodded, stroking the animals. "So you have more work to do," she said softly.

He supposed he did. And for the first time in his life… "I've never not wanted to go back and get a new assignment. I've never…wondered what a different life might look like."

This time when she smiled it was bigger, gentle, but still so sad. "That's because you didn't care if you were alive."

It was true. He hadn't realized it, but it was the simple truth since the day the state took away his sisters and brothers. Since the foster homes kept them apart. His parents were gone, and his siblings taken away from him, and it hadn't really mattered if he'd survive. He'd decided he wanted to put that to good use, and he had.

He'd done good things not caring if he survived them. But today had been different. She'd made it all different. He moved forward. He didn't know what to say or what to do. He didn't know how to be this person she'd made him into.

But he understood, because he knew her, that no matter what he offered, she would find some way to make it…make sense. So, he found a way to scoot his body in between her and her menagerie of animals. Jim wiggled over to him, resting his head in Holden's lap.

Willa leaned over and rested her head on his shoulder, so he wrapped his arm around her. "I care now."

She flung her arms around him then, the cat meowing irritably between them. It was bizarre and somehow…exactly right.

Chapter Twenty-Two

There was no more talking after that. Not of her father, this group that was after her, or the future. Shock and adrenaline seemed to wear off, and everyone staggered off to beds to sleep.

Holden slept with her that night, or rather, morning by the time they'd gotten there. Willa had woken up once and turned into him, and he'd simply held her. They'd held on to each other. She hadn't cried again. She'd simply relaxed back into sleep, tangled up in him.

There'd been no talk of the future then either. Back in the barn he'd said he cared if he lived, but that didn't mean he was going to...what? Stay?

Willa told herself not to wish for it. Just because the danger was over didn't mean Holden's job was over. Dad wasn't out of the woods. Cutting off an arm certainly didn't end any danger.

This time when she rolled over, the spot next to her was empty. She poked her head over the other side of the bed to where Jim had been, but like Holden, he was gone. Jim hadn't left Holden's side since last night. Or this morning.

She squinted at her clock. Seven thirty. And based on the fading light outside her window, seven thirty at night. Oh, her poor animals. What had they been through these past few days? And now she was back and not even taking care of them.

Willa swung out of bed, ignoring the throbbing pain in her head and Pam's irritable meowing. She pulled on a sweatshirt and some thick socks and headed downstairs. She'd tend her animals, try to get her thoughts around what to do about Holden and then maybe have an actual talk with her mother about…everything.

Her heart pinched at that. Truth be told, she didn't want to have that conversation. She didn't want…

Well, this. But she had to face it. A lot sooner than she'd like, because when she got to the kitchen, her mother and Shay were sitting at a table, Holden standing behind them with Jim at his feet.

"Hi," Willa said, wishing she'd stayed in bed.

Mom smiled. "Have a seat, sweetheart. We need to talk about some things."

Great. But Willa didn't have a choice, so she slid into a seat across from Shay. She looked up at Holden, but his expression was blank. Unreadable. Oh, to have that superpower.

But she had emotions, and she'd never wanted to learn how to school them that much.

"First, your mom called the hospital, and your father's prognosis is pretty good. He came out of surgery, and the doctors believe he'll make a good recovery."

When Holden delivered that news, there was some spark of…him. Warmth. But then Shay began to talk.

"Willa, your mother, Holden and I have had some conversations about what the future looks like."

"Without me," Willa noted.

"You were asleep," Holden pointed out.

Willa glared at him. "You could have waited."

"We could have," Shay agreed, with a conciliatory note to her voice. "But there were some time-sensitive things North Star needed to take care of, and it led us to have some conversations about what North Star could do to protect your family."

Mom reached across the table and took her hand. "Yes, we came up with some ideas, but we're not going to force you into anything, Willa. We just…" She trailed off, looking over at Shay.

"North Star came up with a plan," Shay said calmly. "It's been approved by the feds. Holden's agreed. Your mother has agreed. You don't have to. You have an equal say in this, but before being angry about how we came up with the plan without you, why don't you let us tell you what it is."

Willa didn't know what to say or feel, but Shay's calm helped some. "All right."

"In this plan, the North Star tech team would pull the necessary strings to have William, Vera and Willa Zimmerman die in a car accident tomorrow. This will keep those that have your name from coming after you. We *think* we have most of the men with your name currently being processed by the feds, but this is an extra precaution."

Willa looked at Mom. "So, we just wouldn't exist?"

"You'd be dead," Shay said. She was so calm, so straightforward it didn't feel quite as crazy as it should. "Which means your farm would go up for auction. A nice young couple named Holden and Harley Parker would purchase the farm, to live in with Holden's mother, Reeva Parker." Shay nodded at Willa's own mother. "There'd be no connection to who you were, and you wouldn't have to leave. We can create whatever kind of cover we need for Holden so he wouldn't have to be here 24/7."

24/7. Because Holden was still an operative. Not… hers.

"What about…" Willa didn't know how to bring up Dad. She didn't know how not to.

"A man by the name of Josh Parker, Holden's father and Reeva's estranged husband, will be placed in a psychiatric hospital. Should he recover, it's very possible he could join you here," Shay continued in her very bland tone.

Willa felt like her mind was whirling in circles. They were going to fake kill her off. Like a soap opera. Except this wasn't some brand-new identity she was being given. Not exactly.

"But it's your name," Willa said, staring at Holden. He was giving her family his *name*.

"Holden Parker doesn't exist and hasn't since I joined North Star." He shrugged. "It's a good enough name to give."

Willa pushed out a breath. "I don't know what to say."

Mom cleared her throat, and Shay pushed back from the table. She nodded at Holden, and without a word, they left the room so that it was just her and her mother.

"Mom…"

"I know this is a lot. But I'd hoped… You'd still have this place. You'd still get to be you. It would give your father and I a chance to quit in a way we've never been able to." Mom's eyes were shiny with tears, but they didn't fall. She squeezed Willa's hand fiercely. "I want you to be safe, and I want you to have what we couldn't give you before. This does that. But if you don't want it…"

"I want it. I do." They were giving her the life she'd always wanted. Separate from what her parents were. "Would you quit?"

Mom nodded. "I told Shay that I could help her group as a kind of consultant if North Star ever needed it, but I don't want to be in the field anymore. Not after…" She swallowed. "Your father has been unraveling for a while now. I didn't know how to stop it. I didn't know how to get us out. So I just kept pressing forward, hoping something would… get better. I'm sorry it took…this. But this is what he needs. To be out."

"He tried to kill us."

This time a tear did fall over Mom's cheek. "I know. And I know he would have done it. He was… so lost. So broken. The stress of what we'd done…

He couldn't handle it, and I can't... Oh, Willa, I know it's awful. I wish I could be angry, but I'm only sad."

Willa swallowed at her own lump and nodded. "Me too. He wasn't...him. Even when he was fighting me, it was like I was fighting someone else."

Mom nodded. "So, with this plan, he gets help. And maybe he comes home. Maybe he doesn't. I can't think that far ahead. I just know...when you love someone, you figure it out. I love your father. I... I know he would have killed us. I don't know how to reconcile that. His brain let him down. It couldn't bear the weight of the stress any longer. I saw it coming, but I just kept hoping..." She shook her head. "We'll get him the help he needs. One step at a time."

One step at a time. Willa took a deep breath. "Okay. I'll do it."

"I don't want you to do it just for us. Just for him. I want—"

"Mom, I love you. And Dad. And this place. And in this scenario, I get everything I love, everything I want." She thought of having Holden's name. But would she have him?

One step at a time.

"We'll do it. We'll become new people and have new lives." Willa smiled and squeezed her mother's hand. "And we'll be together. There's nothing I want more than to have that."

HOLDEN FELT LIKE Willa had been inside forever. Shay had gone to her room to check in on Sabrina's progress. Holden had needed fresh air. The stars.

He paced the porch, Jim at his heels. Waited forever and ever. When Willa finally came outside, Holden felt like his nerves were strung so tight they'd snap. But he'd made his choices, hadn't he?

She looked down at Jim, watching Holden's every move. "You have a devotee."

"Yeah, he's all right."

She smiled at that.

Ever since Shay had brought to him her plan to give Willa and her family new identities, he'd had a plan. She could have what he'd lost. A family with his name. He'd give it to her willingly. He'd protect her with everything he was, even if it was simply a name.

But it was bigger than that, and he didn't know how to tell her. Didn't know how to…explain anything. Which was why he ended up sounding like an idiot.

"We, uh, have to get legally married. I mean, the tech team is going to forge it, but it'll be…a legal thing even though we didn't…"

She cocked her head and studied him. "I've never seen you quite so nervous."

He straightened. "I'm not nervous."

"You seem very nervous about legally marrying me via forged document."

He sighed. "Well, you're back to your normal self." *Thank God.*

She smiled up at him. "I'm getting there."

She stood there in the evening dark, haloed by the lights on inside the house. Her house. *Our house.* She was…like no one he'd ever known. She'd chained him to a bed. She'd fought him. She'd survived all this and could still…smile. Even after she'd cried.

There were things in front of them that wouldn't be easy, but that didn't change what he felt. What he wanted. "I love you."

"That sounded less nervous."

"Damn it, Willa."

"I think I'm Harley now."

He pulled her to him, because she was toying with him and he probably deserved it. "You're still Willa. You'll always be Willa. You're safe now." He let out a long breath, framing her face with his hands, careful of the bandage. "I want to make us work, I do. But I have to go. Sabrina's trying to stop a hit man from taking out the name your mother gave us. She's like…my sister. If I can help, I have to."

Willa nodded, wrapping her arms around his neck. "But you'll come back."

"If you want me back."

"We're going to be married, as far as I can tell, so you kind of have to."

"It's not real. I mean, it's real, but… You can have that life you wanted. Where you talk to the lady at the post office and have friends and… You might find there's someone better suited to—"

"I won't find you out there, and you're who I want. Maybe it's soon and fast, and maybe we'll find out something that can't be overcome. But I doubt it. Because I love you, and when you love someone, you choose… You choose to figure it out."

Choose. That was a word that hit him hard. "I

didn't get to choose when I was a kid. Losing my parents. My siblings. I didn't have a choice in any of that. I think I went through life without making any real…choices. Not the kind you build your life on. Because you're right, I didn't care if I was alive. At best, I cared about doing a little good in the world, but that was only at best."

"Your best is pretty good, Holden Parker."

He didn't realize he'd needed to hear that. Needed someone to say, out loud and to his face, that he'd done okay.

"Go. Help your sister. Then come back to me, and Jim. In one piece."

He lifted her hand to his mouth and pressed a kiss to her palm. "I promise."

That was a promise Holden kept.

* * * * *

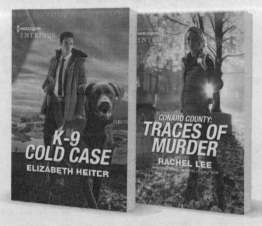

HARLEQUIN

*Uplifting or passionate,
heartfelt or thrilling—
Harlequin has your
happily-ever-after.*

With a wide range of romance series that each
offer new books every month, you are sure to
find the satisfying escape you deserve.

**Look for all Harlequin series
new releases on the
last Tuesday of each month
in stores and online!**

Harlequin.com

#2007 SAFEGUARDING THE SURROGATE
Mercy Ridge Lawmen • by Delores Fossen
Rancher Kara Holland's hot on the trail of a murderer who's been killing surrogates—like she was for her ill sister. But when Kara's trap goes terribly wrong, she's thrust headlong into the killer's crosshairs...along with her sister's widower, Deputy Daniel Logan.

#2008 THE TRAP
A Kyra and Jake Investigation • by Carol Ericson
When a new copycat killer strikes, Detective Jake McAllister and Kyra Chase race to find the mastermind behind LA's serial murders. Now, to protect the woman he loves, Jake must reveal a crucial secret about Kyra's past—the real reason The Player wants her dead.

#2009 PROFILING A KILLER
Behavioral Analysis Unit • by Nichole Severn
Special Agent Nicholas James knows serial killers. After all, he was practically raised by one and later became a Behavioral Analysis Unit specialist to enact justice. But Dr. Aubrey Flood's sister's murder is his highest-stakes case yet. Can Nicholas ensure Aubrey won't become the next victim?

#2010 UNCOVERING SMALL TOWN SECRETS
The Saving Kelby Creek Series • by Tyler Anne Snell
Detective Foster Lovett is determined to help his neighbor, Millie Dean, find her missing brother. But when Millie suddenly becomes a target, he finds himself facing the most dangerous case of his career...

#2011 K-9 HIDEOUT
A K-9 Alaska Novel • by Elizabeth Heiter
Police handler Tate Emory is thankful that Sabrina Jones saved his trusty K-9 companion, Sitka, but he didn't sign up for national media exposure. That exposure unveils his true identity to the dirty Boston cops he took down...and brings Sabrina's murderous stalker even closer to his target.

#2012 COLD CASE TRUE CRIME
An Unsolved Mystery Book • by Denise N. Wheatley
Samantha Vincent runs a true-crime blog, so when a friend asks her to investigate a murder, she's surprised to find the cops may want the case to go cold. Sam is confident she'll catch the killer when Detective Gregory Harris agrees to help her, but everything changes once she becomes a target...

Desparre, Alaska, was so far off the grid, it wasn't even
listed on most maps. But after two years of running and
hiding, Sabrina Jones felt safe again.

She didn't know quite when it had happened, but
slowly the ever-present anxiety in her chest had eased.
The need to relentlessly scan her surroundings every
morning when she woke, every time she left the house,
had faded, too. She didn't remember exactly when the
nightmares had stopped, but it had been over a month
since she'd jerked upright in the middle of the night,
sweating and certain someone was about to kill her like
they'd killed Dylan.

Sabrina walked to the back of the tiny cabin she'd
rented six months ago, one more hiding place in a series
of endless, out-of-the-way spots. Except this one felt
different.

Opening the sliding-glass door, she stepped outside onto the raised deck and immediately shivered. Even in July, Desparre rarely reached above seventy degrees. In the mornings, it was closer to fifty. But it didn't matter. Not when she could stand here and listen to the birds chirping in the distance and breathe in the crisp, fresh air so different from the exhaust-filled city air she'd inhaled most of her life.

The thick woods behind her cabin seemed to stretch forever, and the isolation had given her the kind of peace none of the other small towns she'd found over the years could match. No one lived within a mile of her in any direction. The unpaved driveway leading up to the cabin was long, the cabin itself well hidden in the woods unless you knew it was there. It was several miles from downtown, and she heard cars passing by periodically, but she rarely saw them.

Here, finally, it felt like she was really alone, no possibility of anyone watching her from a distance, plotting and planning.

Don't miss
K-9 Hideout *by Elizabeth Heiter,*
available July 2021 wherever
Harlequin Intrigue books and ebooks are sold.

Harlequin.com

HIEXP0621

Get 4 FREE REWARDS!

We'll send you 2 FREE Books plus 2 FREE Mystery Gifts.

ROOKIE INSTINCTS
CAROL ERICSON

CRIME SCENE COVER-UP
JULIE MILLER

Harlequin Intrigue books are action-packed stories that will keep you on the edge of your seat. Solve the crime and deliver justice at all costs.

FREE
Value Over **$20**